False
Positive

False Positive

FICTION BY **HAROLD JAFFE**

FC2
Normal/Tallahassee

Published by FC2 with support provided by Florida State University, the Unit for Contemporary Literature of the Department of English at Illinois State University, the Program for Writers of the Department of English of the University of Illinois at Chicago, the Illinois Arts Council, and the Florida Arts Council of the Florida Division of Cultural Affairs

Address all inquiries to: Fiction Collective Two, Florida State University, c/o English Department, Tallahassee, FL 32306-1580

ISBN: Paper, 1-57366-098-1

Library of Congress Cataloging-in Publication Data

Jaffe, Harold.
  False positive : fictions / Harold Jaffe.-- 1st ed.
      p. cm.
  ISBN 1-57366-098-1
  1. Current events--Fiction. I. Title.
  PS3560.A312 F3 2002
  813'.54--dc21
                                        2001004519

Cover Design: Victor Mingovits
Book Design: Nicole Gallmann and Tara Reeser

Produced and printed in the United States of America
Printed on recycled paper with soy ink

for G. L.

Books by Harold Jaffe

False Positive..(fiction)

Sex for the Millennium.............................(extreme tales)

Straight Razor.......(stories; visuals by Norman Conquest)

Othello Blues..(novel)

Eros Anti-Eros...(fictions)

Madonna and Other Spectacles.......................(fictions)

Beasts..(fictions)

Dos Indios..(novel)

Mourning Crazy Horse.......................................(stories)

Mole's Pity..(novel)

The American Experience: A Radical Reader......(editor)

Affinities: A Short Story Anthology.....................(editor)

Acknowledgements

A number of these fictions were published in the following journals or anthologies: *ACM*; *Fiction International*; *Kung Avantzine* (Italy); *Loompanics*; *Obscure Publications*; *Shincho* (Japan); *Speak*; *Tattoo Highway*; *two girls review*; *Trepan*; *Western Humanities Review*.

I'd like to thank R.M. Berry, Stephen-Paul Martin, Lance Olsen, Lidia Yuknavitch, and Gayle Luque for reading and commenting on this volume in manuscript.

Author's Note

Each text in *False Positive* was initially a newspaper article which I have "treated." I enter the article, and by various stratagems expose the host text's predictable but obscured ideology, in the process teasing out its most fertile (that is to say, terrorist) subtexts. Thus rearmed, the prosthetic text is released into Culture to do its dirty work.

Contents

YOWL

Geeks Dream

Heather-Jeanne confesses to having felt the urge, imagined the moment, even permitted herself the purely hypothetical pleasure of stabbing a tormentor in the throat or pushing him off a cliff, *zap*, out of her life.

"I totally understand," says the pert, red-haired sophomore at New Hampshire's Portsmouth High School.

"I think everyone has that moment when they think about killing someone."

"It's a rush."

Heather-Jeanne by no means

By no means condones the coldly calculated slayings of 12 students and one teacher by two armed-to-the-teeth, black trench coat-wearing teens at Columbine High School in Littleton, Colorado, on April 20, Adolph Hitler's birthday.

But like a surprising number of young people across the nation, she sees the massacre through the prism of someone who was once, she says, "a mega-geek, one of the total outcasts" in her high school.

For all the revulsion, anger and hatred directed at the Columbine High School killers, the two members of the so-called Trench Coat Mafia have become overnight objects of empathy—sometimes even sympathy—among young people who consider themselves social misfits, forced to the fringes of their peer groups.

Although these teens are of course horrified by the slayings, they tend to blame the cliquish subcultures of what they characterize as uncaring school systems, rather than the two youths who went on their obscenely violent

Their obscenely violent rampage.

The vast communities of Internet chat rooms and bulletin boards have been pulsing with I-told-you-so and that-could-be-me posts.

Several teens openly admitted to identifying with Dylan Klebold and Eric Harris, who police say took their own lives at the end of their psychotic stroll through the suburban Denver high school.

"These two geeks were pushed so far over the edge that they used their only instinct left as a defense mechanism," wrote one youth on a school violence bulletin board.

"Watch out—I could snap next," he added ominously.

Another wrote: "So in the fullness of their love they killed a bunch of bleeping gizmos. So bleeping what!"

At New York City's Norman Thomas High School, Tennessee transplant Cory Abdur-Rahim leaned against a graffiti-defaced wall on an inner city basketball court, long-fingered hands in his jeans, and talked about the social gauntlet a newcomer has to run when he or she arrives at a tough school in a big city.

"I could understand it," Rahim, a whippet-thin ninth grader, said of the frustration.

"Everybody gets picked on, and some people, they take it too far.

"But I could definitely understand it."

The killings in Littleton and a half-dozen school shootings the previous year throughout the country have become something of a Rorschach blotter for people to read what they want into what's wrong with America in general—and its kids in particular.

Easy access to exotic weapons.
Hyper-violent video games.
Shocking song lyrics.
The anything-goes Internet.
Street drugs like crack and ice and *Ecstasy*.
Permissive parenting.
A bad batch of DNA.
The demonic tug of the Millennium.

Although each of these has been considered a culprit to varying degrees, the leading indicator of choice for the moment is the old high school caste system that lumps kids into cliques with Darwinian callousness.

At least until graduation, after which the high school star quarterback may well be offering to check the oil in the geek's fire-engine

Geek's fire-engine red Ferrari.

Yet some ethics watchdogs believe the Revenge of the Nerds theory does not fully explain how one designated dork becomes a schoolmate-slaughtering psycho.

While another morphs into Microsoft multi-billionaire Bill Gates.

And if history is any guide, the more we learn about the Colorado case, the more theories—and laws—will be offered as answers.

To fit any number of political agendas.

F. Roland Plantz is a Michigan State University Professor of Criminology and Ethical Behaviorism who has studied gang culture and youth violence for 17 years.

Dr. Plantz maintains that the massacre in Littleton is symptomatic of a broader erosion of civic values ranging from elected officials seducing their interns to raging motorists shooting each other on the freeways to inner-city "gangstas" wearing the severed ears and genitals

Ears and genitals of their victims as trophies.

Moreover our depersonalized, highly competitive culture compels parents to insist that their kids go the whole nine yards, not take a back seat to anyone, whether on the playing field, in the classroom, or in the social arena.

"It's all about getting what's yours, payback," Professor Plantz points out.

"And with the easier availability of weapons, the conflicts have naturally become more deadly."

Plantz draws a parallel between the hopelessness felt by some suburban "geeks" marginalized in their schools and by poor black or colored youths marginalized by society in general.

"Most marginalized people will make a reasonable adjustment to compensate," Plantz says.

"A smaller percentage will become violent, either to others or themselves."

Plantz asserts that a lack of parental involvement in kids' lives, along with schools that could care less about incorporating ethics

About incorporating ethics and civic values into their lesson plans, are bigger culprits than a violent, bordering on out-of-control, profit-crazed entertainment media.

Statistics show that much of the discussion leading up to a teen mass murder occurs on the Internet, according to Dr. Plantz.

Thus parental involvement would reasonably include becoming computer literate, even constructing personal websites.

As Dr. Plantz puts it, "You don't have to be a rocket scientist to construct a website."

But if individual parents simply lack the facility to construct a website all they have to do is consult their Yellow Pages to locate a federally-licensed Internet technician.

Mass murderer Klebold, on his personal website, boasted about his collection of Nazi memorabilia and openly vowed to murder fellow students at Columbine High, even singling them out by name.

But neither of his parents knew how to surf the Web.

Surf the Web.

Dr. Plantz also emphasized the obvious but often overlooked point that parents should have their children psychologically evaluated twice yearly, if at all possible.

In the instances of Eric Harris and Dylan Klebold, each of the teens had been diagnosed with Attention Deficit Disorder and prescribed Ritalin.

Although Klebold's stepmother said that she had the impression her stepson was spitting out the Ritalin after her back was turned.

According to the autopsy report, neither teen had traces of Ritalin in his body.

Malik Williams, a senior at Strom Thurmond High School in Johnston, South Carolina, says he has "sympathy to a point" for the Columbine killers, even though they purportedly targeted at least one student just because he, like Malik Williams, was black.

"If African Americans could put up with the prejudice that happens every single day, these white guys from the Trench Coat whatever

"Trench Coat whatever could have dealt with their thing without killing," Williams said.

Yet for all the brutality of the crime and the neo-Nazi proclivities of the two killers who timed their mass murder to fall on Adolph Hitler's birthday, the tragedy has at the same time become a rallying point for "geek pride."

Dee Dee Price, a West Virginia high school student who exchanged e-mails with a reporter but wouldn't identify her hometown, said vandals sprayed "death to jocks and preps" and "Trench Coat Mafia" on her school's volleyball court after the killings.

By third period, hundreds of students had gone home, and officials ended up closing school before noon "because everyone in school was shitting their pants,"

"Shitting their pants," Dee Dee Price said.

At a website called Slashdot—"News for Nerds"—the dialogue over the shootings was voluminous and passionate.

Wally Cox of Boston talked about how he often was beaten up or called a "freak" or a "drama fag" during his years at Sacco & Vanzetti High School in the early '90s.

One of his friends was "beaten bloody one night by a whole truckload of jocks, then sodomized with a drum major's baton," he claimed.

"A kid I knew from study hall offered to sell me a Taurus 9mm semi-automatic with a 17-round clip."

Young Cox fantasized about walking through the halls of Sacco & Vanzetti High, holding the Taurus in a two-handed grip, arms rigidly extended, turning left, then right, "blasting to shit everyone who ever kicked my ass, made fun of me, or ignored me.

"I'd need a whole lot of ammo, but I would make them all pay.

"One thing stopped me.

"I couldn't cough up

"**Couldn't cough up** the sixty-five bucks," Wally said.

At Slashdot, Internet surfers complained about a post-Littleton trend of "geek profiling"—compiling databases on kids who have taken on some of the coloration of the Colorado killers.

One self-confessed geek surfer, Heldon (Zook) Teckler, from Texarkana, Texas, said that just because he dyed and spiked his hair, pierced his nipples and scrotum, mutilated his fingers, wore all black, and had a swastika tattooed on his forehead, Charles Manson style, he was "gang-banged to within an inch of my life by a posse of Afro

"**Posse of Afro**-American basketball players, and they were all 6-6 or bigger.

"They were fuckin' huge, man."

Adam R., from Mount Fury High School in Moscow, Idaho, said that during a discussion of the mass murders in his social studies class, he remarked that while he could never condone any killing, he "could, on some level, understand these kids in Colorado, the killers."

After the class, he was called to the principal's office and told he had to undergo seven counseling sessions or face expulsion.

Seven was the maximum allowable number of sessions underwritten by Kaiser Permanente

By Kaiser Permanente, the school district HMO.

Heather-Jeanne now says that although she understands why someone would be driven over the edge by tormentors, she no longer considers herself a geek.

Since she began taking Paxil, a prescribed antidepressant and anti-panic medication four-and-a-half months ago, she has found herself relearning to smile, transcending cliques, and making friends with different types of people.

"People finally realized that I wasn't weird just because I didn't have the money to buy a lot of cool

"Lot of cool clothes."

Severed Hand

Left Hand

A man who cut off his left hand because he thought it was possessed by the devil is suing a doctor and a hospital for $7.5 million for following his instructions not to reattach it.

Huntz Hall contended that medical experts should have known he was psychotic and incapable of making an informed decision after he severed his left hand with a power saw.

Hall's law team, headed by controversial prosecuting attorney Lonnie Parnell, said micro-surgeon Dr. Krishnan Lingam and Sentera Hillcrest General Hospital should have ignored Hall's ramblings and obtained a court order to reattach the hand.

Left Brain

*Lonnie Parnell —is he the self-styled country law-
yer that's always on Larry King Live? Shoulder-length
dyed blond hair. Cheekbone implants. Wears a rawhide jacket and black mock turtleneck. Married a
bunch of times. Wears that strong cologne.*

I can't say about the cologne, but that's the guy.
Parnell.

*So was it only Huntz Hall's left hand that was pos-
sessed by the devil?*

Evidently.

What about his right hand?

No.

What about his left foot?

No.

What about his left big toe?

Don't be a dick, okay?

[pause]

*What was his left hand doing that got it possessed
by the devil?*

Rubbing and squeezing himself improper is what
I heard.

You mean . . .

Exactly.

So he was rubbing and squeezing with his left hand exclusively?

He was using his right to punch the keys. Stroke and point the mouse.

He was online? I had a feeling.

He was trolling through the brackish pornographic backwaters of the World Wide Web.

I heard you can access any perversion a demented mind ever conceived in those backwaters.

I'll hold off comment on that one.

[pause]

So old Huntz would work himself over with his left hand while punching the keys and stroking the mouse with his right?

Sometimes he'd use both hands to punch keys, but the mouse was exclusively right.

Seems like his right hand stroking and squeezing the mouse would be as reprehensible as his left hand squeezing and stroking his—

That's not how he saw it, okay?

[pause]

Odd name: Huntz Hall.

Uh-huh.

Wasn't there a Huntz Hall movie actor? One of the Dead End Kids? Funny-looking horse-faced guy, very comical. Sidekick to Leo Gorcey, who is a story in his own right.

This is a different Huntz Hall.

Recite his particulars.

Thirty-eight. Five-feet-eleven with unnaturally long arms. Fallen arches. Divorced. Actually annulled. After three-and-a-half years. His wife testified that he wouldn't perform the sexual act with her.

Wouldn't or couldn't?

Wouldn't.

How come?

She said he said he wasn't in the mood.

Did he follow professional sports?

Wrestling. The fake shit. Watched it on TV. When he wasn't trolling the Net. He loved that shaved-head guy with all the steroids. Goldberg.

Go to church?

Not since he was a kid. Called himself agnostic.

Constipated?

You mean . . .

Bowel movement. Was he regular? Was he fruitful?

I believe he was irregular. But don't hold me to it.

[pause]

Tell me about his family.

They lived in Chula Vista, south of National City, close to the Mexican border. Parents were Pentecostals. Father worked in the food industry, mother worked part-time as a checker in Lucky. Both dead now. Huntz Hall's only sibling, a sister, converted to Judaism. Orthodox variety.

You're joking.

No.

What's her name?

Who?

Huntz Hall's sis?

Used to be Lavinia Hall. They called her Queenie. She changed it to Zipporah. I think that's Hebrew.

[pause]

Now that Zipper—What's the name?

Zipporah.

Now that she's an orthodox Jewish person I guess she don't live in Chula Vista any more.

After four years in a childless marriage in Chula Vista, she got divorced. She converted to Judaism and moved to Woodstock, NY. She lives in some kind of commune or kibbutz-type setup in the mountains up there.

Janis Joplin's Woodstock?

That was in another life. Besides, the brassy, bluesy boozehound is dead and gone.

So what's happened to Woodstock?

All kinds of competing religious cliques there. Orthodox Jews, militant Muslims, panting Pentecostals, renegade Roman Catholics, simmering Sufis, bumptious Buddhists.

What are they bumptious about?

About the way the shit's flying.

[pause]

You say they compete—these religious cults? How?

Cliques, not cults. They compete with chains, knives, power tools, Uzis, pipe bombs, anti-personnel mines, sharp-edged stones, rusty hubcaps, broken Coors Lite bottles.

Has ESPN or FOX gotten wind of any of this? It'd make some great millennial TV: **Winding Down the Century: The Snuff Games of Woodstock!**

But who'd sponsor it?

Yahoo. Or maybe Pfizer. They're the Viagra folks.

Not bad.

So what happened to Huntz Hall's severed left hand?

Wondering when you'd come to that. They recovered it, but it was too late. All chewed up.

Dog?

After Huntz Hall severed his left hand he chucked it through an open window, right? There are conflicting versions about what happened next. One party claims to have seen a raccoon slinking across Utah Street near where Huntz Hall lived in a furnished studio with the bloody, severed left hand in its jaws. Another party insists that a Rottweiler with a custom latex collar was slobbering all over the severed hand.

What's your theory?

Between the raccoon and the Rottweiler? I'd pick the Rot. Hands down.

[pause]

So what's Huntz Hall doing right now? As we talk?

Being treated with electroshock. You're sticking out your lip. Electroshock is not the barbaric modality it was in your time. For some patients it's a rush, like bungee jumping. If electroshock don't fly, the mental folks may opt for psycho-surgery which they do with lasers now. In and out, no mess.

I'm sticking out my lip because I'm hungry. When we're done here let's do lunch.

Chinese?

Nah.

Thai?

How about Mexican?

Mex is too heavy for lunch. California cuisine?

That'll work.

[pause]

While Huntz Hall is undergoing this electroshock, he's pretty heavily drugged, I imagine.

Oh, sure.

Thorazine?

Among other agents.

What about his severed hand?

If he wins his case against Dr. Krishnan Lingam and Sentera Hillcrest General Hospital, first he'll pay off Lonnie Parnell and the rest of the legal team. Which ain't gonna be cheap. Then he may be able to afford a prosthesis. Not one of those steel claws like in your time. These are state-of-the-art, electronically managed "hyper-hands" composed of a flesh-like synthetic. They're supposed to be as good as flesh and blood. Some experts claim they're better.

Will his electronically-managed hyper-left hand work as well in the squeezing and stroking department?

That's a dead issue. Whether it's electroshock, lasering his frontal lobe, mega-doses of meds, or distributing his mania into a software program, Huntz Hall won't be rubbing and squeezing himself anymore. Bank on it.

Distributing mania into software? What's the deal?

Employing computer technology on behalf of our soon-to-be-interfaced species.

Homo sapiens?

Homo-techno-sapiens. You look skeptical.

If I was skeptical about the infinite potency and fundamental decency of high-technology, you'd make a citizen's arrest. I know you.

[pause]

One last thing: The devil that possessed Huntz Hall's left hand—does s/he have her/his own website?

Yes, s/he does. You satisfied, motherfucker? Let's do lunch.

Carthage, Miss.

A 9-year-old boy whose mother died at home lived with the corpse for a month, fixing his own meals and attending school without fail because he was afraid he'd be put in foster care if anyone found out.

A 9-year-old boy whose mother purportedly died at home lived with the corpse for a month, fixing his own meals and attending school without fail, because he was, by his own admission, afraid he'd be put in foster care if anyone found out.

When Crystal Wells died on Nov. 3, her son Travis draped her denim jacket over her body, covered her face and shoulders with newspaper, and laid her, face up, in a corner of the cramped family room of the one-bedroom trailer.

When Crystal Wells died on Nov. 3, her son Tyler covered her body with her pale mauve terrycloth bathrobe, placed sheets of toilet paper over her face and shoulders, and set her, face up, in a corner of the cramped family room of the one-bedroom trailer.

Crystal was petite, just five-feet-one in her stocking feet.

Crystal was petite, just five-feet-two in her lizard skin line-dancing boots.

After his mom's death, Travis prepared meals—mainly frozen pizza, Froot Loops and beef jerky—and went to school every day until her body was discovered Monday by family friends Dot and Earl Begley.

After his mom's death, Tyler fixed his own meals— mainly frozen pizza, chocolate energy bars and chunky style peanut butter—and went to school every day until Crystal's body was discovered Monday by her half-sister and brother-in-law, Dot and Earl Begley.

Unable to contact Crystal, Dot and Earl Begley drove to the trailer park.

Unable to contact Crystal, Dot and Earl drove their metallic green '84 El Camino to her trailer, stopping on the way at the liquor store.

Travis answered the door.

Tyler answered the door.

"At first he said his mom was at work and wouldn't let us inside," Dot said.

"At first he said his mom was sleeping and wouldn't let us inside," Dot said.

"When we asked again, he changed his story and said she was gambling over there at the Indian casino. Barona."

"When we asked again, he changed his story and said she was visiting his uncle Jeep, in Mobile. Jeep's real name is J.P. Cotton. Everyone called him Jeep."

"When we asked a third time he finally just broke down and said, 'Mama can't talk no more because she got real sick and I think she is dead.'"

"When we asked a third time he just broke down and said, 'Mama can't talk no more because she got real sick and I think she is dead.'"

Dot Begley said Travis begged them not to call the police.

Dot Begley said Tyler begged them not to call the police. "I asked him why not. He said because they were fat-assed homophobic yahoos."

Travis told them he lived with the body on the family room floor because he was afraid of being placed in a foster home.

Tyler told them he lived with the body on the family room floor because he was afraid of being seduced and abandoned.

Despite Dot and Earl's testimony that the cramped one-bedroom trailer stank, Travis insisted that his dead mom's body did not smell.

Despite Dot and Earl's testimony that the cramped one-bedroom trailer reeked, Tyler insisted that his dead mama's body did not smell.

Police have not released a cause of death for Wells, 30, but said foul play was not at this time suspected.

Police have not released a cause of death for Wells, 32, but said foul play was not at this time suspected.

However, rumors have been circulating that a marauding Negro who'd just escaped from a chain gang was being investigated and that an arrest was imminent.

However, rumors have been circulating that a homeless drifter who called himself Count was being investigated and that an arrest was imminent.

Chain gangs have reappeared in several deep south states after a recent ballot amendment promoting chain gangs was approved by nearly 80 percent of the electorate.

Chain gangs have reappeared in several deep south states after a recent ballot amendment promoting chain gangs was approved by nearly 80 percent of the electorate. Of course, only 19 percent of the electorate voted.

Dot Begley said Travis told her that after his mother died he would take the bus to school, buy a mango smoothie, do his homework and surf the Internet.

Dot Begley said Tyler told her that after his mom died he would take the bus to school, smoke crack in the boys' room, do his homework and troll the Internet.

Police computer experts have reviewed Travis's bookmarks but have not yet released their findings.

Police computer experts have reviewed and analyzed Tyler's bookmarks but have not yet released their findings.

However, rumors continue to swirl about the boy's penchant for deviant sex, which he downloaded from the Net and saved as bookmarks.

However, rumors continue to swirl about the boy's penchant for perverted sex, which he downloaded from the Net and saved as bookmarks.

And now there is the additional suggestion that Travis, who is sexually precocious, met an older male via a chat room on a homosexual porn site.

And now there is the additional suggestion that Tyler, sexually precocious, met an older male via a chat room on a homosexual porn site, and that this male may have interfaced with Crystal, Tyler's mom, when she was still alive.

When Travis ran out of food he walked to the 7-Eleven and bought more, Dot Begley reported.

When Tyler ran out of food he skateboarded to the 7-Eleven and bought more, Dot Begley reported.

For now, Travis will live with his maternal grandmother, Luddy Hadley, in Carthage Miss., as her temporary ward.

For now, Tyler will live with his maternal grandmother, Luddy Hadley, in Carthage Miss., as her temporary ward.

Luddy Hadley's husband, Virgil, had been convicted of child abuse and murder 12 years ago and was sentenced to two life terms in prison. While taking his weekly shower, he was attacked by other inmates wielding razor-sharp soup spoons.

Luddy's husband, Virgil, an ungainly male with jug-shaped ears, had been convicted of child abuse and murder 14 years ago and was sentenced to two life terms in prison. While taking his bi-weekly shower, he was attacked by tattooed inmates wielding razor-sharp soup spoons.

Virgil Hadley was brutally sodomized then stabbed 28 times.

The ungainly male child-abuser with jug-shaped ears was viciously gang-raped then stabbed 37 times.

Afterwards, one of the assaulting inmates was alleged to have said that plugging Virgil Hadley was like thrusting his fist into a sewer drain.

Afterwards, one of the tattooed perpetrators said that Virgil Hadley was the raunchiest bitch he'd punked since being sent up twenty-something years ago.

American prison inmates are notoriously intolerant of child abusers.

American prison inmates are notoriously intolerant of child abusers.

Now there is indisputable evidence that deviant sexuality is chemical, located in the brain; that it is conveyed on the y, or male, chromosome.

Now there is unassailable evidence that perverted sex is chemical and hereditary, conveyed on the y, or male, chromosome.

Which doesn't bode well for Travis.

Which ain't exactly good news for Tyler.

Bodybag

Black dude. They say he killed some folks.

What they give him?

12 death sentences.

Man!

Plus 9 life sentences.

Musta been some hard-assed judge.

Plus 322 years for a bunch of other crimes they say he done.

These sentences are to be served consecutively?

Concurrently.

That's what I meant. Musta been white folks he snuffed.

Yeah. Except he denies it.

Alibi?

His sister says he was home playing checkers.

Playing with who?

Hisself. Solo. His sister said that's what he liked to do.

I guess he lived with his sister.

Her and her family. She pretty much supported him.

He didn't have a job?

He couldn't hold a job. They said he was slow.

You were at the arraignment, right? Did he look slow to you?

He looked all right to me.

Did his sister look slow?

No.

Did the judge look slow?

The judge looked like an old white man with thin lips, watery blue eyes, and long hands with liver stains on them. He kept rubbing Chap Stick on his lips.

I guess he was an old white man with thin chapped lips.

Uh-huh.

[pause]

What was wrong with his alibi?

They didn't believe it. They thought she was just sticking up for him because she was his sister and he was slow. After the O.J. thing, they want to make sure they don't cut black suspects too much slack. Don't let black suspects get to juking them. Like O.J. did.

What happens if he's innocent?

Then an innocent black man gets executed by lethal injection.

Executed 12 times by lethal injection.

Hell, they have enough venom to inject him 12 times. Inject his homeboys 12 times too.

Inject his homeboys' homeboys.

Uh-huh.

[pause]

It ain't the prison's fault.

What?

I said it ain't the prison's fault.

Hell, no, they just want to make a living. And if they make a killing, so much the better.

Who?

The prisons. They're like any other self-respecting economic entity. They want their capital gains. And they want their profit.

[pause]

So they gave him 12 death sentences, 9 life imprisonments. And what else?

322 years.

Can he appeal?

To who?

A higher court. Ain't that how they do it?

He's got 3 strikes.

I didn't know that. What's that mean?

Dead doo.

[pause]

How's he feeling?

You mean . . .

The condemned black guy with his 3 strikes, 12 death sentences, 9 life imprisonments, plus 322 years.

How would you feel?

I'd feel shitty. Fucked over. Pissed on from a great height.

Whole lot of piss, right?

Ton of piss.

[pause]

Is he playing checkers?

Funny you ask. That's about all he does do. He won a death row round-robin in Pelican Bay. Now he's petitioning to take the tournament to Quentin. If he wins there, to Folsom.

If he wins at Folsom?

Corcoran. That's where the finals are at.

He plays mano-a-mano?

No. These brothers are all on death row which means they ain't permitted to see a human being. When he makes a checker move he transfers it to a sound signal. The signal is conveyed through a computer to the competing prisoner.

Each checker move and series of moves has a sound signal which he talks into a computer?

Uh-huh.

Have you heard them? How do they sound?

Like shrieks and stabs of pain.

[pause]

So I guess there are none of those conjugal visits . . .

He's under 24-hour observation. Can't even jack off. Not that he'd want to.

What you're saying, I think, is solitary on death row at Pelican Bay ain't all that sexy. What does he eat?

Muslim-type chow. When they give it to him. He's studying Islam and wants to become a Muslim.

Studying from . . .

The Koran. That and the Bible are the only books they allow.

What about TV?

He got him one. Old black and white.

Which is good for those old gangster flicks.

He only gets one channel.

[pause]

When's he scheduled to get his lethal injection?

Today's Tuesday, the 8th?

Today's Thursday, the 11th.

 The 28th. 17 days from today. 6:30 a.m. That's when they give him his lethal injection.

After they do him?

Tag his big toe, stuff him in a bodybag. The California DOC bodybag is specially constructed to hold weight and fluids without leaking.

What does DOC mean?

Department of Corrections.

And the bodybag is specially constructed? Constructed where? Mexico? The Philippines?

Constructed by inmates in the California prisons.

I guess they can get pretty raunchy.

What?

Bodybags.

Well, yeah.

So what happens next?

They drop the bodybag containing the freshly executed black male in the morgue. Morgue dudes check him out and cut into his body. See if they can harvest his organs.

Organ transplants is a major growth industry.

Damn right.

[pause]

What happens to the bodybag?

The . . .

Bodybag. What happens to it?

Stored in the prison storing area with the other bodybags till they need to use it again.

Uh-huh.

Sometimes they sell it.

Sell the raunchy bodybag? Who to?

Museums, galleries, performance groups, Internet auction houses. Death and shit are big $$$ now. So are colored folks. Art & entertainment.

Glendale & Palmdale

A female driver forced a male in another car off a remote mountain road Friday.

Hacked him to death beside the highway.

Urinated on his corpse.

Then fled in his car, witnesses said.

The attacker screamed obscenities at the male before lunging at him with a butcher's cleaver, according to the witnesses who called 911 from a nearby tavern.

Authorities were tight-lipped about the 2:50 p.m. attack on Angeles Forest Highway in Angeles National Forest between Glendale and Palmdale.

But the following details emerged.

Los Angeles sheriff's deputies were searching for a creme or beige four-door sedan, possibly a Taurus or Toyota Camry, said Deputy Jacki Ramer.

The car was last seen speeding toward Glendale.

Ramer said investigators had not identified the victim or the killer, but that they were working on several leads.

She said at least two sets of people witnessed the attack and were expected to be interviewed by detectives.

The suspect was described as white.

Blonde.

Muscular.

Heavily tattooed.

Wearing an emerald tongue stud and wraparound mirror shades.

She was in her late 20s.

Alva Lewis, owner of the Hidden Springs Tavern, said two males who had been bird watching observed the attack through their binoculars.

They tried to contact authorities from their cellphone, but, unaccountably, the cellphone malfunctioned.

So they called authorities from a pay phone outside Lewis's restaurant, about three miles from where the attack occurred on a desolate stretch of the two-lane forest highway.

The witnesses reported seeing a cloud of dust and two cars screech to a stop on the side of the road.

The muscular female leaped out of her car and attacked the male.

The witnesses reported that the attacker had a Sig Sauer 9mm pistol and that she stuck the barrel in the male's mouth.

Then she yanked him partially out of the driver's seat window and, producing the butcher's cleaver, hacked him to death with "rapid, powerful blows."

The bird-watching witnesses told Deputy Ramer that the killer then dropped her jeans, pulled aside her black thong panties and urinated on the hacked-up male.

According to the same witnesses, she peed standing up, "like a man does."

Next she calmly lit a Marlboro, and with the cigarette in her mouth, pulled the hacked-up, blood-soaked, pissed-upon male corpse through the window and dropped him on the rocky turf.

She slid into the cockpit of the dead male's creme or beige Taurus or Camry and sped off in the direction of Glendale.

"I don't think it was random or road rage or anything like that," Ramer said.

"She swore at him when she got out of the car.

"She lit a Marlboro.

"She urinated on him.

"These two individuals knew each other."

Alva Lewis, who has run the Hidden Springs Tavern for nearly three decades, said such violence is rare in the almost uninhabited reaches of the national forest.

"Usually folks murder someone down in the city and bring them up here to dump them," she said.

"We've never had anything like this here happen before."

**

An elementary school teacher who had a baby by one of her sixth-graders has pleaded guilty to rape of a child.

Marie Beth Hermanson, a 35-year-old mother of four other children, made her plea Thursday.

She could get up to 10 years in prison at sentencing Aug. 29.

She said she still has feelings for the boy—who turned 14 a month after their daughter was born in May—and wants to raise the girl he fathered.

The two met when she taught his second-grade class in this Seattle suburb.

"There was a respect, an insight, a spirit, an understanding between us that grew over time," Hermanson told *The Seattle Times* earlier this month.

By the time he was in her class again, in sixth grade, "he was my best friend," she said.

"We just walked together in the same rhythm."

Hermanson and the boy began having sex last summer.

After she got pregnant, her husband informed relatives, one of whom contacted school officials and social workers.

Hermanson has since lost custody of her four children—ages 3 to 12—and her husband has filed for divorce.

The boy is in counseling.

"He's doing fine as long as he's away from the situation and people don't harass him," said his mother, adding that he still loves the teacher.

The boy is Samoan.

**

A male driver forced a female in another car off a remote mountain road Friday.
Slashed her to death beside the highway.
Changed into her bloody clothes.
And fled in her car, witnesses said.

The attacker screamed obscenities at the female before lunging at her with a straight razor, according to the witnesses who called 911 from a nearby tavern.

Authorities were tight-lipped about the 2:40 p.m. attack on Angeles Forest Highway in Angeles National Forest between Glendale & Palmdale.

But the following details emerged.

Los Angeles sheriff's deputies were searching for a reddish or burgundy two-door coupe, possibly a Saturn or Nissan Altima, said Deputy Jacki Ramer.

The car was last seen speeding toward Palmdale.

Ramer said investigators had not yet identified the victim or the killer, but that they were working on several leads.

She said at least two sets of people witnessed the attack and were expected to be interviewed by detectives.

The suspect was described as a white man in his thirties.

Burly.

Tattooed.

Head shaved.

With a fire-engine red goatee and wraparound mirror shades.

He wore a swastika-shaped gold or gold-plated earring in his left ear.

Alva Lewis, owner of the Hidden Springs Tavern, said two females who had been bird watching observed the attack through their binoculars.

They tried to contact authorities from their cellphone, but for reasons still unclear the cellphone malfunctioned.

So they called authorities from a pay phone outside Lewis's restaurant, two miles from where the attack occurred on a desolate stretch of the two-lane forest highway.

The witnesses reported seeing a cloud of dust and two cars screech to a stop on the side of the road.

The male hurtled out of his car and attacked the female in the other car.

The witnesses reported that the attacker first used a large caliber Smith & Wesson revolver to pistol-whip her about the head.

Then he yanked her partially out of the driver's seat window and, producing a straight razor, slashed her repeatedly.

According to the witnesses, the killer then withdrew a ten-inch Cuban cigar, admired it, sniffed it, and calmly lit it with a lighter.

A rich, thick cloud of smoke issued out of his nose and mouth.

With the Cuban cigar in his mouth, he pulled the dead female through the window and dropped her on the leafy turf.

Next he dropped his jeans and shorts, pulled off the dead female's blood-soaked jeans and black thong panties, and snuggled into them.

Dripping blood and viscera, he squeezed into the cockpit of the female's red or burgundy Saturn or Nissan Altima coupe and, with the Cuban cigar still in his mouth, sped off in the direction of Palmdale.

"I don't think it was random or road rage or anything like that," Deputy Ramer said.

"He swore at her when he got out of the car.

"He put on her bloody jeans and black thong panties.

"He lit a Cuban cigar.

"These individuals knew each other."

Alva Lewis, who has run the Hidden Springs Tavern for nearly three decades, said such violence is rare in the almost uninhabited reaches of the national forest.

"Usually folks murder somebody down in the city and bring them up here to dump them," she said.

"We've never had anything like this here happen before."

Faux

Reese Luginbill was just another white male with uncooperative veins to a hospital worker who had trouble drawing blood at his bedside.

She had no idea who Reese Luginbill really was.

After she finally obtained a vial of his blood, the worker accidentally tossed it into a can of used needles and other medical waste and then dumped the can into a sink to retrieve the blood sample.

She left the mess behind for Luginbill to clean up.

When he protested, she belched coarsely and said: "Shut your trap. This is my house."

Luginbill secretly recorded and videotaped the exchange.

The hospital worker, who turned out to be a chronic patient-abuser, was summarily dismissed, fined and incarcerated in a voter-approved, freshly erected penal institution for women.

For his part, Reese Luginbill was a prominent member of an emerging breed called "faux patients," hired by hospitals or private watchdog agencies to feign illness and assess the way patients are treated.

With hospitals, physicians, administrators and health-care impresarios vying for patients in an increasingly profitable and competitive medical marketplace, growing numbers are spying on themselves to see how they can improve their product.

Similarly, the prison industry, which in the last half-decade has increased its profitability thirty-fold, enlists faux prisoners to assess how it can improve *its* product.

In truth, the boards of prisons, banks, medical institutions, the biotech industry, theme parks and major universities tend to include the self-same "suits": Caucasian, market-minded technocrats with top-flight MBAs.

The employment of faux shoppers is a familiar research technique for stores, banks, restaurants and theme parks.

But the ruse is more difficult to pull off in a hospital.

Not just anyone can check in.

And not just anyone is willing to be prodded, poked with needles, patronized, molested, infected, ignored and massively X-rayed all for the sake of research.

And a paycheck, of course.

The best and boldest faux patient will go right to the brink of surgery, and occasionally beyond, to test the strengths and weaknesses of a hospital or physician's office.

"It's not like sending someone to Burger King or McDonald's or Nordstrom," asserted W. Lauren Barbieri, a consultant from La Jolla, California, who runs a national network of faux patients and frequently goes undercover herself.

"To do it in a hospital is a very complex undertaking."

Faux patients must be superior actors able to simulate the appropriate symptoms.

Face and body makeup may have to be applied.

Phony lab results may need to be prepared.

And at least one physician and hospital administrator must be enlisted in the ruse to ensure that the incognito investigator will be admitted.

Their collusion naturally costs $$.

Which is ultimately passed on to the consumer, that is, to the true patient.

Polls indicate that consumers, increasingly critical of their HMOs, are willing to pay higher hospital costs provided the service is improved.

In one case Lauren Barbieri, her body hair shaved clean, went all the way to the brink of major organ surgery before the surgeon (who was part of the plot) made up an excuse to cancel the procedure, saying Barbieri had drunk a mimosa (California-brand champagne and orange juice) that morning.

An absolute no-no for patients who are surgery scheduled.

Sidebar: It turned out that Lauren Barbieri liked not having body hair and has maintained that "waxed" look, augmenting it with three strategically placed piercings.

Other experiences are more mundane.

Reese Luginbill recalls being forced to stand for nearly an hour in a fake full leg cast while he checked in at one group practice.

"Registering patients while they are sitting or laying down went against their hospital procedure," he pointed out.

"Those little things, they're what make people angry.

"Which could mean they will look for another medical provider.

"Which is obviously a negative from the management standpoint."

Faux patient Renee Cruz-Bosworth's specialty is scoping out dentists.

The promotional brochure on her website shows her wearing a floor-length mink and a Lone Ranger-type mask to avoid blowing her cover when she arrives for a check-up or other dental care.

"I've got super-clean teeth," laughs the Dallas-based consultant.

"I've had 'em straightened,

"Had 'em whitened,

"Had 'em bonded."

Still, she goes back for more, a secret microphone taped to the inside of her thigh and a Japanese-made miniature camcorder secreted in her nipple ring.

Bosworth also brings her own X-rays to avoid over-exposure to radiation.

Hospitals and physicians agree that having faux patients test their service can help busy administrators understand how patients feel as they wind their way through the often bewildering health care network.

For example, Reese Luginbill's visit at Banner Royall Hospital in Cleveland, Tennessee, brought new attention to little things, like making sure aides empty bedpans within 24 hours.

Or turn patients' wheelchairs around in the elevators so they are not stuck facing the wall.

Or respond to a terminal patient's summons in the middle of the night.

"Small things mean so much," said Banner Royall's marketing director, F. Brandon Dewayne.

He labeled Luginbill's visit "the sentinel event" in a succcessful but ongoing effort to improve his hospital's service.

"Good as we are, there's always room for improvement.

"That's what our investors expect of us.

"Or of any industry in which they have placed their trust."

Consumer advocates claim they do not know much about faux patients, but they welcome the idea of medical professionals trying to find out more about how patients feel.

"It's a gut check for the health care industry," said Rich Reiker of Families USA, a consumer group.

Suzanne Sargent-Vail, spokesperson for the American Hospital Association, said faux patients can provide useful—but limited—information.

"You can never truly have the point of view of the patient," she explained.

"You're missing the most important factors: pain, discomfort, extreme alienation, risk of infection, gnawing fear and death itself."

Sargent-Vail did concede that the undercover investigators can offer insights on "hotel-type" issues such as courtesy, food and responses to special requests.

The experience does not come cheap.

Reese Luginbill, who's been a faux patient "30-something" times over the past five years, charges $18,000 to $25,000 plus expenses for what is usually a three-day hospital stay.

(Selective discounts are available to repeat abusers.)

Faux patients report they have little trouble maintaining their cover, but Reese Luginbill did find himself on the receiving end of the deception once when, after a few single malt scotches, a physician in the know tipped off the radiologist that Luginbill was a faux patient.

The radiologist, a wag in his own right, decided to play a trick on Luginbill and told him that there was a suspicious spot on one of his X-rays which could be a malignant tumor.

He had Luginbill sweating bullets for nearly a week before he 'fessed up.

Reese Luginbill wasn't impressed.

"Sure, I was a faux patient," Luginbill admitted, "but cancer is not funny."

**

Jumpin Cop and Candy 3D were a couple of flirters in the weird, faceless and soon-to-be-utterly-capitalized frontier of Internet chat rooms.

But when their dialogue grew lurid it entered the world of digital dirty talk: stuff unfit for a family newspaper.

Later they graduated to cell phone sex.

Through it all, Candy 3D made it pretty clear to Jumpin Cop: She was 13-years-old.

Jumpin Cop now claims he didn't believe her.

And now jurors are trying to determine if they believe Jumpin Cop, the Internet pseudonym for a real cop: Redondo Beach police officer Randy Spielman, 46.

The 22-year police veteran and father of two teen-aged daughters was arrested last year and indicted on two counts of attempted lewd acts on a child and a single count of attempted sending of harmful material.

He was nabbed in a Redondo Beach Police Department sting in which computer-proficient officers log on to the Internet pretending to be teens or adolescents.

Sprawled provocatively on their virtual perch, the pretend-teens wait expectantly for the lewd come-on from adults.

Candy 3D was the online moniker for an odd couple of Redondo Beach detectives: Horst Lockman and LuEllen Gomez, of the RBPD's Sexually Exploited Child Unit.

Lockman, 39, the actual creator of Candy, is a heavy smoker, weighs 312 pounds and speaks in a croaky bass, while Gomez, 36, is five-foot-eight and sinewy, with an adolescent's high voice.

Though Jumpin Cop Spielman was indicted for attempted lewd acts on a child, obviously neither Detectives Lockman nor Gomez is a child as such.

In real time.

Spielman's trial began this week and is expected to go to the jury Monday.

If convicted, he faces five years behind bars and the loss of his taxpayer-funded job.

Spielman currently is assigned to a neighborhood policing unit, a department spokesperson said.

Besides embarrassing the veteran officer, the case is being viewed as a litmus test regarding law enforcement's use of the pseudo-anonymous world of Internet chat rooms to entrap potential pedophiles.

Funded by an anonymous donor, Spielman has hired Lonnie Parnell, the celebrated defense attorney.

Parnell is the flashy Larry King favorite, with his signature swept-back white perm, black silk mock turtleneck and tawny rawhide jacket.

Parnell contends that his client assumed Candy 3D was an older woman masquerading as a 13-year-old.

"Internet activity consists of people playing roles and representing themselves to be other than they are; that is its *modus operandi*," Parnell argued in court papers.

But yesterday, Deputy District Attorney Rob Balthus presented the jury of seven women and five men with transcripts of the online chats between Jumpin Cop and Candy 3D.

In each encounter Candy cleaved to her fictional age of 13.

"Are you really 13? Man!" Jumpin Cop typed in as they conducted a one-on-one conversation over the Internet carrier America Online on Oct. 15, 1998.

They chatted again four days later.

"How old are you, for real?" Jumpin Cop asked again.

"Thirteen, for real," Candy 3D replied.

"Whoa."

"Why whoa?"

"I better keep you a secret."

"How come?"

"Someone might think I shouldn't talk to you."

"Who cares?" Candy said.

"I care if it gets my butt in trouble," Jumpin Cop responded.

On November 18, Spielman chatted a third time with Candy on AOL and asked for her phone number.

Unbeknownst to Spielman, he was given a special RBPD number, and when he phoned, police officer LuEllen Gomez picked up the receiver.

Gomez turned on her high-pitched adolescent Candy 3D voice.

Jumpin Cop and Candy 3D engaged in a 20-minute phone conversation that was replayed in court.

It left at least one alternate juror wrinkling her cosmetically repaired nose in apparent disgust.

During the conversation, Spielman repeatedly asked Candy 3D to "touch" herself, even as he was, according to his own terminology, "jacking off."

During the same conversation, Gomez, as Candy, told of being molested by an uncle and liking it, and said she was looking forward to meeting Jumpin Cop.

Candy 3D described herself to Spielman as under five feet tall.

"Man, you're tiny," Spielman said.

"Yes, but I'm only 13, remember! How tall are you, Jumpin Cop?"

"I'm 6-4, Candy."

"And I guess you're hung like a horse, right?"

Jokingly, Jumpin Cop snorted.

Then he whinnied.

As the sexual nature of the call intensified, Detective Gomez said, "My mom just came back from bingo," and she hung up.

As the tape played yesterday, Spielman focused his bloodshot eyes on the judge's bench.

Detective Horst Lockman testified that he used various features available on America Online to create an identity for 13-year-old Candy, who listed her hobbies as "nude skateboarding, lingerie modeling and large dogs."

A "personal quote" rounding out the profile said, "Bigger is better, and older guys are bigger than boys."

The Internet service includes a search feature that allows customers to find people who share common interests.

Lockman speculated that Spielman used this feature to find Candy.

Within days of her creation, Candy 3D was contacted by Jumpin Cop through a one-on-one chat function of the AOL program.

Lockman and Gomez testified that they never initiated any conversations, that Spielman started them all.

"It was a stakeout," Lockman said.

"We just waited."

Lockman also testified that police found a handful of downloaded pictures of "girls" stored on Spielman's computer.

Lockman said he believed the ages of most of those pictured were between fifteen and seventeen-and-a-half.

At the center of Spielman's defense is an electronic message he sent to Candy the day after their phone-sex encounter, in which he explained that he thought she was older than 13.

"One of the fun things about AOL is that you can 'play' with a variety of people and allow imagination to run free," stated the message, which defense attorney Parnell theatrically recited in court.

"A great example is a friend back east," Jumpin Cop's electronic message via Parnell continued.

"Dude used to come on as a 15-year-old girl and play games.

"He was actually 59 years old and recuperating from a quadruple bypass."

Spielman, according to Parnell, then proceeded to tell Candy 3D that while he didn't think she was 13, he believed she was under 18, hence "totally outside my limits."

"I enjoy playing role games online but I would never carry it out in real time since it would not be moral, or legal for that matter," Spielman said.

"Sorry, you sound real sexy," Jumpin Cop concluded in his e-mail. "But it's better I stay away."

Spielman did not testify in his own defense, but Parnell called two teenage girls and a 20-year-old female, all friends of Spielman's daughters, Michelle and Monique.

The defense witnesses testified in turn that Spielman never did anything sexually improper in their presence, and that, to them, he seemed like a "real good dad."

The final witness for the defense was Internet consultant and best-selling author Jackie Phillips, who testified that it was common for people to misrepresent themselves when they chat online.

"The medium is the message," Phillips declaimed. "And the medium of the Internet chat room is all about masking, game-playing, fantasizing, having a hoot, squeezing your mouse, getting into a zone, going the whole nine without hurting anyone in real time."

After a pregnant pause, Jackie Phillips added dramatically: "As long as you keep your fingers on your **own** mouse."

The courtroom erupted in laughter.

Mad Cow

An agro-terrorist arrives in the nation's capital armed with a deadly weapon obtained by scraping off lesions from the blistered tongue of an African cow with hoof-and-mouth disease.

A Normal Heights man who engaged in lewd conduct with horses was ordered to stay away from all livestock—and from the entire population, animal and human, of Normal Heights—for three years under an unusual probation sentence handed down yesterday.

With several million particles of virus stored in a lunch cooler, the agro-terrorist rents a Glacier Pearl (that's a color) Nissan Maxima at the Avis counter in Dulles International Airport outside Washington and drives south into the lush Virginia countryside.

Richard Milhous, 42, a delicately built male with a greying mustache, also was ordered to undergo counseling and to pay $1,750 in fines and restitution.

The agro-terrorist stops his Maxima at targeted corporate farms where cattle or horses stand propped up in cramped cages. Using wads of cotton, the agro-terrorist calmly rubs some of the hoof-and-mouth virus into their nostrils. By the time he reaches historic Richmond an epidemic is underway.

Throughout most of yesterday's 90-minute hearing, Milhous sat at a defense table with his left hand shielding his face from the more than three dozen Normal Heights ranchers in attendance, most of whom wore white or black Stetsons.

If this hypothetical terrorism had actually occurred, the $54 billion-a-year US dairy and beef industry would have been in turmoil, international trade would have been crippled and thousands—maybe tens of thousands—of cattle, horses, pigs and poultry would have to be destroyed. It would take years to sort out all the economic and political repercussions.

Several ranchers—including San Diego Wild Animal Park spokesperson Cheryl Nuttall—told Municipal Court Judge Wade W. Richter that Milhous had been sneaking into their corrals late at night for years and "bothering" their stock animals.

Bio-terrorism aimed at humans would "economically pale" in comparison with an attack on American agriculture. The billion-dollar dairy industry would be devastated by "mad cow" disease, Asian longhorn beetles would be used to kill maple trees, crippling syrup production in New England and a virulent soybean rust would wipe out an $8 billion-a-year industry.

Nuttall testified that she witnessed the defendant engaging in "perverse behavior" with one of her mares.

Valuable livestock and poultry are especially vulnerable because most serious diseases that affect them have, at least within US boundaries, been eradicated by science. As a result, American stock animals lack the antibodies to combat the agro-terrorist's chemical agents.

"I'm going to have to assume that you do not have control over your impulses," the judge told Milhous, ordering him to abandon Normal Heights at once, to stay at least 300 yards from livestock, and 100 yards from any animal larger than a full-grown squirrel.

Moreover, stock animals are now fed intensively: some feedlots comprise 100,000 inhabitants, and large congregations make ideal targets for the agro-terrorist's infectious agents. If a biological attack were made as animals were being shipped to slaughterhouses, disease could spread wildly, making it nearly impossible to contain.

Asked if he would comply, Milhous responded: "I have no choice, do I?"

Experts worry that agro-terror may be more attractive than traditional biological or chemical attacks because it presents less risk to the perpetrator.

His other choice, the judge said, was eighteen months in jail and the likely prospect of having his body hair forcibly shaved and being repeatedly gang-raped by fellow inmates.

The United States currently has no means to detect and thwart such an attack, according to biological warfare experts. "We're incredibly vulnerable," said Drew Pendleton, an FBI special assistant who oversees an elite hazardous materials unit that responds to terrorist actions.

Richard Milhous pleaded guilty May 13 to one misdemeanor charge of lewd conduct.

"Agro-terrorism gets the terrorists' murderous point across while not necessarily crossing the threshold of killing people, thus doesn't create the same kind of backlash," said one terrorism expert.

Charges of trespassing and sexual assault were dismissed as part of the plea bargain.

While most experts say biological terror against humans demands at least some grasp of molecular biology, targeting animals can be done by comparatively low-tech means. Which means in effect that any moron with a grudge and a mustache can mount a devastating terrorist attack against our multi-billion-dollar agriculture industry.

Milhous's attorney, public defender Marylou Kim, criticized the probation conditions as excessively harsh. "My client does not hurt the horses," she told the judge. "He happens to have a deep affection for animals."

Pavel Vinogradov, a leading Russian germ-warfare official who defected in 1992, has provided the US government with chilling details of an actual agro-terrorist project that was uncovered at the last minute in the former Soviet Union. Code-named **Ruble,** the terrorist project developed variants of diseases to attack cattle, pigs, chickens and ermines.

"We're talking about a human being," public defender Kim reminded the judge. "We think it's unreasonable

*that the court ask him to stay away not only from all
livestock but from domestic animals as well."*

These highly poisonous agents were designed
to be sprayed from tanks attached to aircraft and flown
low along a straight line for hundreds of miles. Even if
only a few creatures were initially infected, the conta-
gion would wipe out livestock over a wide area in a
matter of weeks.

*Several ranchers reported that their horses behaved
"strangely" after what they described as Milhous's trespassing late-night visits.*

Vinogradov's disclosures were a wakeup call
to government officials who had ignored agriculture
in mapping their counter-terrorism protocols. Now Agriculture Department officials are hoping to persuade
Congress to fund a counter-agro-terror program.

*One rancher, Paiute Luna, testified that she hired a pri-
vate investigator who videotaped one of the encounters.*

Flip Hormel, a top USDA official spearheading
this effort, noted ruefully that there is no deterrent in
the form of punishment for agro-terrorism, in contrast
to nuclear, chemical or biological attacks that kill or
injure people.

*"The man needs help and should be kept away from
any kind of animal, large or small," Paiute Luna told
the judge.*

"There was a national effort on human-centered
terrorism with some significant funding from both the
public and private sectors," Flip Hormel explained. "But
the USDA and Agriculture got the short end of the stick.
Now it's catch-up time."

When, afterwards, Paiute Luna was asked if she was satisfied with the sentence, she nodded her head but said she did not think Milhous would abide by it. Then she put on her black Stetson, adjusted her chaps, and left the premises.

Zealous Hysterectomies

A floating army of zealots roams mid-Asia in search of regimes to overthrow.

The appearance of Islamic insurgents in **Qa** just days before the Millennium has not only shocked regional leaders and their Russian and Chinese neighbors, it has awakened the civilized world to a disturbing new phenomenon: the existence of a floating army of fanatically religious warriors roaming this part of the world in search of regimes to lay waste.

Qa is one of eight new nations that emerged in Central Asia and the Caucasus following the collapse of the Soviet Union in 1991. The region is poor, deprived, bereft, unstable, virulent and populated by Muslims and tribes people.

But it sparkles like a glittering jade for religious zealots.

The fanatical warriors who suddenly materialized in mid-December have their roots in the extremist Islamic Taliban sect of Afghanistan. They pose a grave threat to stability in a vast area that stretches from Turkey's eastern border all the way to China.

Reportedly the extremists have withdrawn to bases in the mountains around Kabul and in neighboring **Pk**, freeing hostages along the way, many of whom were mutilated in torture.

Their withdrawal is strategic. Not a soul believes they will lay down their weapons and relinquish their dream of bringing the entire region under religious rule.

Visions of Attilla, the Scourge of God? Title this ragtag, rapidly metastasizing army the Scourge *from* God. With Internet savvy.

The Taliban maintain a sophisticated website with Arabic, Uzbek and English variants, slick graphics and convenient pull-down menus. The site is undisguisedly committed to worldwide terrorism on behalf of a fiercely fundamentalist Islam.

As civil war rages in Afghanistan, religious violence has broken out not only in **Qa** but in three other sectors to the north and east.

In **Yp**, officially part of Russia, rabid fundamentalists are forging a violent campaign for independence.

An even more fanatical wing is warring in the neighboring republic of **Ts**, also nominally under Russian sovereignty.

Farther east, the border that separates **Ts** and **K** is temporarily at peace following a bloody conflict in which Muslim zealots played a commanding role.

Ironically, much of the religious militancy fanning through Central Asia and the Caucasus can be traced back to the US campaign to drive Soviet forces from Afghanistan in the 1980s. The Soviet Union hung on in Afghanistan for a decade before retreating with its collective tail between its legs.

Meanwhile the bungling **CIA** was spending hundreds of millions of dollars training native anti-communist fighters and supplying them with postmodern weapons.

Now the same fanatics with the same black mustaches and black intense eyes are using those skills, and in many cases those weapons, to topple "godless" regimes.

Crucial to the religious extremists' long-term strategy has been the systematic destruction of non-Islamic monuments and the erection of mosques, along with money earmarked for the religious "education" of disaffiliated youths.

They have attracted thousands of teenagers and adolescents, who in many instances have no strong religious convictions, but who are captivated by the warrior romance they associate with mythified heroes like Che, Clint Eastwood, Yassir Arafat, Carlos the Jackal and Sly Stallone as *Rambo*, which only recently has shown up on movie screens in these Muslim backwaters.

Drug "tribes", numbering in the scores, recognizing the importance of controlling trade routes through the region, also eagerly contribute fighters.

This motley legion of zealots, children, dopers, reprobates and murderers is sponsored by a murky network of religious and political self-styled visionaries, featuring the Saudi billionaire extremist Osama bin Laden, who now makes his headquarters in Afghanistan.

US authorities say bin Laden, using the latest electronic technology to communicate with his far-flung terrorist supporters, has directed them to strike Americans everywhere immediately following the Millennium.

In the meantime the insurgents have been fomenting microwars in "soft tissue" regions where the strategy is to strike furiously and overwhelm. They have found such targets in **Qa**, **K**, **Ts** and in the Fergana Valley, the heart of Central Asia.

When they retreat, they move back to bases in Afghanistan and also in **Pk**, where fanatically religious warlords have usurped control from the central government.

In **Osh**, one of the main towns in the Fergana Valley, people are bewildered and terrified by the insurgency. Their relatively permissive brand of Islam has been under assault from extremists bivouacked in the hills.

"The situation is very flamable for all of Central Asia," said Bakyt Beshimov, former provost of **Osh** Academy, who now represents this region in the **Ts** parliament.

"Part of the danger is that the insurgents are sponsored by large industries abroad: oil companies, fast food enterprises and hi-technology firms avidly seeking out markets in a densely populated but largely uncharted area of the world.

"The other problem is the degraded social conditions in this region, which, in effect, force people to support violent alternatives."

People across the region have seen living standards plummet since the Soviet Union disintegrated. Once they enjoyed guaranteed jobs, education and health care. Now they are poor, with little prospect for improvement.

"When humans live in misery, the slogans of fundamentalists are very appealing," Beshimov observed. "They are urging Muslims to rise up against the political regimes that are the source of their difficulties. They say they have the formula for a more just society."

Because the regions in question are isolated, western powers have been slow to react. **Ts** prime minister Askar Akayev said that he is now relying on China to "crack the whip. They have to, the insurgents are about to take **Xng**."

Xng is China's westernmost province. But its population is mainly Islamic, and its people feel scant loyalty to Beijing. They are restive, and radicals among them have set off bombs which some experts believe mark the onset of a no-holds-barred separatist campaign.

"I can understand the complacency in the West, since all this seems very far away," said Askar Aitmatov, an adviser to Askar Akayev.

"But fanatical religious fundamentalism is growing like a cancer, and the world had better take notice."

**

Contrary to popular belief, a hysterectomy will not ruin a woman's sex life and often can improve it significantly, a new study asserts.

Most of the 1,132 women in the study reported they had sex more frequently, experienced more and stronger orgasms and had less pain during intercourse *after* undergoing the procedure for non-cancerous conditions.

The findings could allay one of the biggest fears of women who must decide whether to have the surgery.

"If they're worried that a radical hysterectomy will cause difficulty in sexual functioning, our study results indicate the opposite," said Aileen V. Hendry, a University of South Carolina professor of epidemiology who led the study.

Women usually have their uteruses removed because of severe anemia and back or pelvic pain caused by such things as fibroid tumors, abnormal menstrual bleeding and endometriosis, which is excessive growth of the uterine lining.

The sexual problems caused by those disorders are for the most part erased after the radical hysterectomy, according to the study's findings.

Women "simply feel better after the hysterectomy, and sexual functioning improves along with overall health and quality of life," Dr. Hendry explained.

The researchers also said that some women might be getting more enjoyment out of sex because they no longer fear getting pregnant.

The study appears in today's *Journal of the American Medical Association.*

Lots of articles in ladies' magazines and books have taken "a kind of anti-hysterectomy stance" because of the fear of sexual dysfunction, Dr. Hendry said. "But they are simply not based on scientific results."

Critics claim that more than half of the estimated 600,000 hysterectomies performed every year in the US are unnecessary and put otherwise healthy women at risk of serious complications and death.

Dr. Hendry conceded that a hysterectomy "is more serious than a root canal," but that with advanced medical technology, and with the new study's finding of improved sexual functioning, the hysterectomy should be made widely available as a "preventive procedure par excellence."

The researchers surveyed the women before surgery and at 6, 12, 18 and 24 months afterward. Even women with lesser gynecological problems before surgery reported a "definite improvement in their sex lives."

A year after surgery, the number of women having sex at least five times a month increased by 10 percent, and 72 percent of women reported having orgasms, compared with 63 percent before surgery.

Women experiencing pain during sex dropped from 40 percent before to 15 percent two years after surgery.

Dr. Shanda Gluck-Teasdale, an obstetrician and gynecologist at the Albert Einstein Medical School, said she is not surprised by the results.

"I can count on the fingers of one hand the number of complaints I've heard after a hysterectomy," she said.

"I'm gratified that someone is finally proving what we've been experiencing all along in clinical practice."

KALI

Salaam

When the Palestinian terrorist opened his shirt to display the explosives taped to his chest, the Israeli shop owner pointed to a large cast iron pot simmering on the stove. It contained cabbage, potatoes, green onions and—unmistakably—a tiny human hand.

*

When the Palestinian opened his shirt to display the explosives taped to his chest, the Israeli shop owner on the crowded Jerusalem street pointed to the old pot simmering on the stove. Cabbage, potatoes, green onions and a tiny human hand.

The Palestinian was young, slender, with black eyes and the tracings of a black mustache.

The shop owner was wiry with bloodshot eyes and a once black now grey and white mustache.

They glared into each other's eyes.

Then, as the young Palestinian raised his fist, the old man raised his arm with numbers tattooed on it.

The young man pronounced the word *Palestine* even as the old man uttered the word *Auschwitz*.

Each in his own tongue.

*

When the Palestinian opened his shirt to display the explosives taped to his chest, the Israeli shop owner pointed to the large pot simmering on the stove. It contained cabbage, potatoes, green onions and—conspicuously—a tiny human hand.

Palestinian: —I know that hand. It is my sister's hand.

Israeli: —You are wrong. It is my sister's hand.

—The hand is tiny. You are an old man.

—I was young then as you. In another country.

*

—So you are a suicide bomber.

—Freedom fighter.

—Murdering hundreds of anonymous Jews will provide this freedom?

—It is the only way left.

—You have heard of the word genocide?

—Every day of my life I hear this word.

*

When the Palestinian opened his shirt displaying the explosives taped to his chest, the Israeli shop owner on the crowded Jerusalem street pointed to the large pot simmering on the stove. Cabbage, potatoes, green onions and a tiny human hand.

Glaring into each other's eyes.

—What is it that you want?

—The Jews to give us back our land. That we can live in peace.

—And if I tell you that this land in Jerusalem and beyond is not yours but ours. Historically ours.

—Let the United Nations decide.

—And the Jew-haters in the UN. What about them?

*

—You are prepared to murder yourself and hundreds of ordinary people you do not know who happen to be Jews. Why? Because of a principle?

—If this principle means truth, then yes, God willing. I am prepared to join my martyred freedom-fighting brothers and sisters.

—There are many others who feel as you do?

—I cannot give numbers. But I have never met a Palestinian who was not prepared to die for freedom.

—And if you did meet one?

—I would refuse to shake his hand.

*

When the Palestinian opened his shirt and displayed the explosives taped to his chest, the Israeli shop owner pointed to the large pot simmering on the stove. It contained cabbage, potatoes, green onions and—unmistakably—a tiny human hand.

—You Jews are cannibals.

—The opposite is true. We have been cannibalized.

—You are talking about Nazis. You cannot stop talking about your Nazis.

—No.

—That is the problem with you Jews. You live in the past.

—No. We live in the present under the weight of the past. There is no other way.

*

—These Nazis that so obsess you. You have become them.

—What are you saying?

—Just that. You Israelis in your crisp uniforms with your advanced weapons slaughter us and degrade us as the Nazis did you.

—What you are parroting here I have heard before. It has become fashionable. It is an unspeakable slander. And coming from you with genocide taped and strapped across your body!

*

When the Palestinian freedom fighter opened her blouse to display the explosives taped to her body, the Israeli shop owner's daughter gestured to her breast then pointed to the Palestinian's breast.

They gazed long into each other's dark eyes.

Then the Palestinian jerked her head to the side, reached under her blouse, detonated.

That is one version. The other version follows.

After looking long at each other, the Palestinian freedom fighter nodded her head once, slowly.

Carefully, she disarmed the explosives.

Then she and the shop owner's daughter embraced and arm in arm stepped out into the turbulent Jerusalem street.

Karla Faye

Condemned killer Karla Faye Tucker learns today whether Texas parole officials believe she is a reformed female who should be spared execution.

If the Texas Board of Pardons and Paroles rules against the diminutive admitted killer of two, and all other appeals are denied, she would become only the second female put to death in Texas since the Civil War.

The deliberating panel said its decision on Karla Faye Tucker's fate would be announced 32 hours before her scheduled execution tomorrow by lethal injection, which, according to punishment experts, is the most humane method of execution currently available.

Karla Faye Tucker would be the first female executed in Texas since 1863 and only the second in the

US since the Supreme Court permitted capital punishment to resume in 1976.

The 38-year-old former teenage prostitute, drug abuser, biker slut and rock band groupie received the death penalty for killing two people with a pickax in 1983.

The sovereign state of Texas adopted lethal injection as a means of execution in 1977. The electric chair had been employed in Texas from 1924 through 1976. Affectionately called Mr. Zap, it was the original model constructed from Galveston white oak in 1923. Condemned inmates were transported to the state penitentiary in Huntsville where they were forcibly introduced to Mr. Zap.

Karla Faye Tucker asked the 18-member parole board to recommend clemency to Governor George W. Bush, contending she is a reformed female who has found Jesus Christ and can serve as a resource and role model for other abused women if she is granted a life sentence without parole.

Ten board members must agree with her before the governor has the option of sparing her life. But even a single favorable vote would be highly unusual. Of the 23 males who sought clemency in 1997, none received a dissenting vote. Of course these were African American or Latino males, not a petite 100-pound Caucasian female with the face of a madonna.

Lethal injection consists of Sodium Thiopental, Pancuronium Bromide and Potassium Chloride. The process averages seven minutes, 13 seconds, and the cost per execution for the drugs is $86.08.

Karla Faye Tucker has an appeal pending before the US Supreme Court which argues that the commutation process in Texas is unconstitutional, lacking clear guidelines and adequate hearings. If her appeal is rejected, she would be the first Caucasian female with auburn hair weighing less than 163 pounds ever executed in the state of Texas.

A Bush spokeswoman said yesterday the governor would hold off on a decision in the case until the Supreme Court rules. The governor was at his family compound in Maine hunting pheasant with his father, George senior, the former president and architect of Desert Storm, and with his younger brother, Jeb, the governor of Florida and the president and CFO of the Florida Marlins baseball team.

Karla Faye Tucker, who would be the 147th Texas inmate executed since Charlie Brooks (black) in 1982, has admitted using a pickax to kill a 64-year-old Texarkana man named Moseby that she and a male accomplice robbed of $37.14. Tucker then killed the victim's 61-year-old wife to eliminate her as a witness.

Karla Faye Tucker delivered 36 blows to the female victim and 29 to the male. The forensic investigative unit calculated that a single blow would have been sufficient to kill each victim. Tucker was a 171-pound weightlifter with a tongue stud and multiple tattoos when she committed the murders.

Tucker's male accomplice, a full-blood American Indian of the Shoshone tribe, was on death row, awaiting execution by lethal injection, when he was stabbed to death in the shower by a fellow inmate in 1985 as he allegedly resisted being raped. The killer had fashioned his lethal weapon from a soup spoon smuggled out of the prison mess in his ponytail.

The assailant claimed that he merely wanted to massage the victim's prostate as he had done several times before, at the victim's request. Only this time the victim resisted violently and so the would-be prostate masseur killed him in self-defense.

The state of Texas executed its first inmate by electrocution on February 8, 1924. On the same date, six additional inmates were executed in the following order:
Chucky Reynolds (black), Red River County, murder.
Ewell Morris (black), Liberty County, kidnapping.
George Washington (black), Newton County, rape.
Mark Mathew (black), Tyler County, loitering.
Melvin Johnson (black), Liberty County, rape.
Joby Jefferson (black), Harris County, rape.

Karla Faye Tucker now claims she committed the grisly murders under the influence of drugs which were forced on her by her Shoshone Indian male accomplice, who, like her stepfather, when she was a child, sexually abused her. The Shoshone, named Jimmy Fast Horse, had coarse, shoulder-length black hair, a Fu Manchu mustache, multiple homemade tattoos and four self-administered finger and toe amputations.

Karla Faye Tucker claims also to have been gang-raped by Guns N' Roses in her rock band groupie days. The news here, according to Karla Faye, is that Axl Rose and his self-styled baddies were either undersized or flaccid, or both, even with the coke, speed and lord-knows-what they were snorting, shooting and sticking up their butts.

Prison officials were bracing for several thousand news reporters and photographers travelling from as far away as Japan and Zimbabwe with the expectation of covering the first execution of a Caucasian female since 1984, when Velma Jean Barfield was put to death in Florida by electric chair. It malfunctioned; Barfield received third-degree burns on her head and body and it took her 19-and-a-half minutes to be pronounced dead.

Photos of the burnt and bloody Velma Jean Barfield, along with the defective electric chair, called Old Sparky, recently surfaced on a commercial website called *HotGore* coming out of Houston. The webmaster claimed that the grisly photos generated more than three million hits in ten days, which, if true, would be a record, according to an AOL spokesperson who declined to be identified.

Karla Faye Tucker, her attorneys, prosecutors and the governor all insisted her gender should have no bearing on her case. But the tiny, doe-eyed, uncommonly telegenic, computer-literate inmate, has drawn worldwide attention and garnered considerable sympathy, even admiration.

Especially after her highly successful appearance on Larry King Live, which attracted nearly twice as many viewers as the competing Houston Rockets-Chicago Bulls professional basketball game featuring Michael Jordan in his last appearance (in a Bulls uniform) in Houston.

Pope John Paul II initially saw Karla Faye Tucker while trolling through CNN News online. Now he has joined her widening chorus of admirers. In a fax to Texas governor Bush, the Polish-born pontiff asked for "a gesture of clemency which would help create a culture more favorable towards the respect for life," reported the Italian news agency ANSA, quoting Vatican sources.

Longtime Cuban strongman, Fidel Castro, has also voiced his opposition to "this senseless, brutal execution of a severely disadvantaged female whose future was foreclosed by capitalism at her birth," the *Miami Herald* reported, citing official Havana sources.

Two recent Internet polls have shown a narrow majority of Texans do not want Karla Faye Tucker executed, though most of those polled claimed not to care one way or the other, perhaps because of their preoccupation with the Houston Astros, who just captured the division title and are preparing to play the Los Angeles Dodgers, now owned by billionaire entertainment mogul Rupert Murdoch and the Fox family.

Women throughout the US and in several first world countries including Canada, Japan, the UK, France and Germany have rallied to Karla Faye Tucker's defense.

Hotel rooms in Huntsville, a city of less than 30,000, about 80 miles north of Houston, were jacked up to three times their normal tariff—and they were at a premium. One hundred eighty-three special telephone/fax lines set aside outside the prison for media organizations to purchase were gone in two-and-a-half days.

Karla Faye Tucker requested a final meal of a ripe banana, peaches and a tossed salad with bacon bits, with either ranch or Italian dressing. Ranch was her first choice.

Should her appeal be turned down and the execution take place, Karla Faye Tucker has stated that she would not, repeat: *not,* hold a grudge against the Texas Board of Pardons and Paroles or against Governor George W. Bush.

The US Supreme Court declared capital punishment "cruel and unusual" on June 29, 1972, at which time there were 45 men on death row in Texas and 11 in Texas county jails who had been condemned to death. The Governor of Texas commuted all of those sentences to life sentences and death row was cleared by March 1973.

But two months later the Texas Legislature, in plenary session, moved to revise the Texas Penal Code, and effective January 1, 1974, Texas courts began reassessing the death penalty, despite the Supreme Court injunction. Under the new statute, the first man put to death in the sovereign state of Texas was Leonel Herrera (Hispanic) on July 17, 1974.

Karla Faye Tucker requested that ten people view her death, because five is her lucky number and ten is five times two. She also requested that at least three of the viewers be born-again female Caucasians from her hometown of Texarkana.

Fast forward: Karla Faye Tucker's appeal was, as anticipated, unanimously rejected; preparations were made for her execution.

When everyone was seated in the lethal execution chambers, the Warden asked Karla Faye whether she would like to make a final statement. Karla Faye replied: "I would like to say to the Mosebys that I am very, very sorry of depriving you of your mama and daddy. To Warden Taggett and Chaplain Jesse Turner, I thank you very, very much. You been so good to me. To my family and friends that has stuck by me, I love yawl from the bottom of my heart. I am going to be face to face with Jesus now. I will see all yawl when you get up there. I will be dressed in wat."

Pizza Parlor

The wife and mother-in-law of a convicted child molester took him captive, brutalized him sexually, and with a serrated kitchen knife carved "I am a child molester" on his belly before dumping him, wrapped only in a blanket, behind a pizza parlor 93 miles away.

Three females—including the wife's aunt—were indicted Tuesday on charges of kidnapping and raping 27-year-old Rodney Hostetter who was released in February after serving two years in Calapatria State Prison for molesting a 7-year-old child.

The husband of one of the three women also was indicted for allegedly trying to bribe Hostetter to drop the charges.

"I don't know if it was a warning or revenge," Captain Burt Yancey said. "With what was carved on his belly, you can draw your own conclusions."

Jewel Hostetter, 26, her mother Mary Louise Coomey, 44, and Jewel Hostetter's aunt, Velma P. Larmer, 39, are accused of attacking Hostetter July 26 at his rented trailer in this semi-rural family community just north of Spring Valley.

According to police reports, the man was on his back on the couch sipping a Diet Sprite, watching TV when the women burst in, wrestled him to the floor, bound his hands behind his back, pulled off his Reeboks, and cut off his sweatpants and jockeys. They shaved his pubic hair, raped him with a zucchini, rubbed a heat-producing ointment on his genitals and forced the self-styled vegetarian to eat raw hamburger, which he promptly upchucked.

Rodney Hostetter told authorities he tried to resist and was "screaming from the pain."

After carving "I am a child molester" on his belly, the three women allegedly drove him 93 miles to his hometown of Indio, dropping him behind the Pasodoble Pizza Parlor, naked, except for a pink and green Minnie Mouse blanket, with his hands still tied behind his back.

Rodney Hostetter could not be reached for comment yesterday. His phone is unlisted, his fax is out of order, and following the incident, America Online abruptly terminated his e-mail account.

The women face one count each of rape and two counts of kidnapping. Each of the charges carries three to 10 years in prison. However, sentiment in this southern California family community is over-whelmingly in the women's favor and against Rodney Hostetter.

One middle-aged male, father of two adolescent boys, seemed to speak for the citizenry of Spring Valley, and for all of California and much of the US when he said: "I hate child molesters, period. If I was those women I would have cut off his b—s."

14 Questions

1) How long has Rodney the child molester been a vegetarian?

From the outset. Instilled by his parents who were Sixties-era flower children. So even though it may not seem like a big deal, forcing him to eat raw hamburger like the women did got his attention.

2) Rodney Hostetter must be a frail male to let himself be overpowered, stripped, bound, raped with a zucchini and transported 93 miles to the Pasodoble Pizza Parlor naked except for that pink and green Minnie Mouse blanket.

Rodney Hostetter is 5-feet-10, 154 pounds naked except for his earrings, nipple ring and tattoos. He's a halfway decent athlete who played some second base for his junior high school team. Well, maybe he's a little soft. The thing is Jewel Hostetter's aunt Velma P. Larmer is 6-3, 240 and an ex-wrestler on the professional women's tour. She was known as Monstress Velma. She hated Rodney's butt even before he was child molesting.

3) Those two years Rodney Hostetter spent in Calapatria? Did the other inmates fuck him over because he was a convicted child molester?

Nah. That's a myth. Child abuse, molestation, what have you—it ain't no different than carjacking. I imagine he was fucked over some in the joint, but only because he's soft.

4) Which one of them carved "I am a child molester" with a serrated kitchen knife on Rodney's belly? Must've been a lot of blood.

Mary Louise Coomey, Jewel's mom, did the carving. And, yeah, there was a whole lot of red stuff, but the women wore rubber gloves, black long-sleeved sweaters, and black jeans stuck into their black high boots. They looked like freakin' ninjas.

5) So has Rodney the child molester's wife, Jewel, filed for divorce?

Jewel's mom and aunt are pushing her to file, but she claims she still loves him, Rodney. Claims she wants a child with him. Three children as a matter of fact. She wants to raise a nuclear family with him right there in Indio between Orange County and the Salton Sea.

6) They pulled off his Reeboks, cut off his jeans and jocks, shaved his head and pubic hair, carved "I am a child molester" on his belly and raped him with a zucchini. Whose idea was the zucchini?

Mary Louise Coomey, Jewel's mom. She has a green thumb. Which Jewel didn't inherit, by the way. Actually Mary Louise wanted to use a cucumber while Velma P. Larmer wanted to fist him, with the rubber glove on, of course. The two women appealed to Jewel, who couldn't make up her mind. The zucchini was a compromise. The child molester would have been better off with Velma P. Larmer's fist, fat as it is. That zucchini was about as big as a toddler's arm.

7) So they burst into the trailer and Rodney the child molester is on his back on the couch watching TV and sipping a Diet Sprite. What is he, a teetotaler?

Hell, it was 9:45 in the a.m. Rodney likes his brew well enough, but, no, he ain't any kind of a hellish drinker. If you read that as meaning he isn't a manly man, that's your privilege. Again, blame it on his Sixties counter-culture upbringing. In case you're wondering what all he was watching, it was one of them sexy tabloid deals. Either *Montel* or *Oprah*, or maybe that other fatty, I can't remember her name.

8) Why drive 93 miles to drop him behind the Pasodoble Pizza Parlor in Indio? What's the significance there?

93 is a crucial number in Jewel Hostetter's astrological chart having to do with Mars, the moon, Scorpio and the Christian trinity. I don't know all the fine print. Pasodoble was the dance Mary Louise Coomey and her husband, Jewel's dad, were dancing when he popped the question. Pizza with pepperoni, anchovies, meatballs, jalapeños, black olives, mushrooms and, I think, pineapple was what Velma P. Larmer and her husband Leon ate on the night she won the super-heavyweight title on the pro women's tour.

9) What is the significance of the pink and green Minnie Mouse blanket that they wrapped the child molester in?

Couldn't tell you. There are more than a few imponderables in this business, and the pink and green Minnie Mouse blanket is one of them.

10) The husband of one of the three women also was indicted for trying to bribe Hostetter to drop the charges. Whose husband and what was the bribe?

That would be Velma P. Larmer's husband, Leon, her ex-wrestling manager; he's a paraplegic. Trampoline accident when he was in community college. He offered Rodney Hostetter season tickets to the San Diego Chargers home games in exchange for dropping the kidnapping, assault and rape charges. Evidently Rodney considered the offer but then rejected it.

11) What about the rumor that the women were high on speed or crack?

That's a lotta shit, okay? Mary Louise Coomey had drank a bunch of coffee—12 or 14 mugs. But that was her custom. Jewel suffered from clinical depression and was up to 160 mills of Prozac daily. Velma P. Larmer, who's an early riser, had been on her back on a crawler since 5 a.m. working on her custom GMC pickup. It's a long bed. Yeah, she could have been a little stoked from breathing that engine oil and high-octane gas. But none of them were high on speed or crack or any other damn thing.

12) Incidentally, did Rodney Hostetter ever admit to the child molesting charge?

No way. Denied it from the get go. His idea was that he was set up by the child's dad. The child himself had obviously been coached and still wavered on the identification. The judge, in his wisdom, felt there was strong enough evidence to convict. The child's father is an assistant district attorney up there in Twenty-nine Palms.

13) Twenty-nine Palms. Ain't that where that big-ass Marine Corps base is at?

Uh-huh. Second largest Marine base in SoCal. After Camp Pendleton.

14) So what is Rodney the child molester up to these days?

Not much. Does some maintenance around the trailer park. He used to drive part-time for UPS, but after his conviction they wouldn't take him back.

Chesus & the Dead Amputee

A bizarre trial in which a former physician is accused of murdering a New Jersey man by botching the amputation of his healthy leg may *not* be decided by the jury that has been hearing the case for the last week-and-a-half.

The Chula Vista Superior Court judge presiding over the trial surprised the lawyers on both sides by announcing yesterday that he was reconsidering a legal decision he made last week and may have to declare a mistrial today.

Judge Matthew Y. Scoggin, 72, claimed he was having second thoughts about allowing prosecutors to present evidence of previous botched surgeries performed by the defendant, Damian Skelly, also 72.

Skelly, a pale male with thick spectacles, a flattened nose, and uncommonly long fingers, is accused of murdering Bernard L. Samsen, who paid Skelly

$9,075 to sever his healthy left leg to fulfill a nearly lifelong wish to become an amputee.

Samsen, 68, was found dead in a National City motel two days after the May 1998 operation Skelly performed in a Tijuana clinic.

Eight transsexuals, variously pre- and post-operative, were scheduled to testify that they were disfigured in operations by Skelly over a period of almost ten years.

Five of the transsexuals were F2M. Two were M2F.

The physical disposition of the eighth could not be ascertained.

At the onset of the trial, Judge Scoggin, peering over his spectacles, liver-splotched hands clasped in front of his nose, ruled that prosecutor Lynda Torres-Cohen, 41, would be permitted to call the transsexuals to bolster her contention that Skelly knew he was an inept surgeon and was fully aware that he was putting Samsen's life at risk.

Torres-Cohen: faux-blond, ambitious, lipsticky, is said to have modeled her self-presentation on Linda Tripp, of the Clinton-Lewinsky entanglement.

Like her briefly infamous namesake, Torres-Cohen is fond of steak tartare.

Skelly's California state license to practice medicine was revoked in 1978 for incompetence after botching an attempt to transplant a liver from a potbellied pig to a 57-year-old human female.

The pig, called Garth, and the human died within minutes of each other on adjoining operating tables, Garth expiring first.

Skelly also spent 13-and-a-half months in Calapatria State Prison early in the decade after being convicted of practicing medicine without a license.

In prison Skelly was routinely sodomized.

One fellow inmate, who resembles ex-President Clinton's rakehell half-brother Roger, allegedly said that plugging Skelly was like thrusting his fist into a sewer drain.

The record shows that Skelly acquired home-made tattoos.

Including one, above his coccyx, of a naked genderless human, back to front, with the left leg sound and the right a thigh-stump.

This could not be immediately verified.

Prosecutor Torres-Cohen addressed the jury at the start of trial regarding the transsexuals, employing graphic details of the ordeals they were alleged to have suffered because of Skelly.

Her technical assistant, as she referred to him, a very tall black male with a shaved head and theatrically deadpan manner, projected lurid slides of bloody, botched cross-gender surgeries on the wall.

He referenced each slide in a mellow Billy Eckstine bass.

Torres-Cohen addressed the technical assistant as O.G.

One had the impression that with a little nudge O.G. would have launched into song.

Dance too, if it came to that.

As these things go, it was an impressive performance.

However, late yesterday afternoon, after the jury had been dismissed for the day, Judge Scoggin, according to his custom, had a dram of Bushmills single malt Irish and took a nap in his chambers.

When he awoke with a snort fifty-three minutes later he had changed his mind about admissible testimony.

Whether his change of mind was provoked by a dream, nightmare, dybbuk, incubus, succubus or garden-variety Irish gremlin, he did not specify.

The judge informed the lawyers that if he decided this morning not to allow the transsexuals' testimony, as he was now inclined, he would consider granting a mistrial.

Torres-Cohen, visibly upset, animatedly argued her position.

"How the heck else do I show the jury [Skelly's past behavior and conduct]?

"Your honor, it's the heart and soul of my case.

"It's the history, the baggage, the whole dang shooting match.

"He knew he shouldn't've come within spitting distance of a scalpel or a saw or a butcher knife or whatever the heck he used.

"You've heard of dope, booze, sex addiction.

"This freak is addicted to mutilating live bodies.

"It's a turn-on for him.

"For his own good and the good of the community, he's got to be put away."

Judge Scoggin was unmoved.

He repeated his comments about declaring a mistrial after a full day of testimony by a Delaware man, Jungian psychoanalyst Drake Marston, 66, who was a close friend of Samsen and shared the same amputation fetish.

Marston, tall, emaciated, with lank hair the color of egg salad, testified that he paid Skelly to amputate his own left leg last year but backed out at the last minute.

Contributing to his change of heart, Marston said, was observing the Mexican doctor who was to assist Skelly during the surgery walk into a Tijuana medical clinic, chewing a strip of beef jerky while carrying a large serrated butcher knife under his arm.

The Mexican doctor, according to Marston, wore a strong cologne.

Marston also testified that it was he who sought out Dr. Skelly's services, that Skelly never pressured him to have his left leg amputated.

Nor did he locate Skelly through an ad on an X-rated amputee website, as was alleged.

Rather he found him indirectly, through word of mouth.

Twelve days after Marston decided against surgery, his friend Samsen flew via US Air into Chula Vista and used the $5,500 deposit Marston had paid Skelly as a down payment for his own amputation, the court was told.

Under questioning by defense lawyer Phillip R. P. Kost, 47, Marston said he never would have let Samsen go through with the surgery had he thought his friend would die.

Kost, six-feet-three and stooped, resembles the Anglican-Royalist poet T.S. Eliot, who along with his sometime-friend, the volatile Pound, has made an inestimable contribution to American letters.

Kost acquired his law degree on the Caribbean island of Grenada.

He was there when Ronald Reagan sent in the Marine Corps to root out Creole communism.

Marston testified that Samsen, a slight male with a large head and wizened child's face, was "delighted" the night after his leg had been amputated.

In his elation Samsen sang the lyrics of "Fly Me to the Moon" in a robust tenor, according to Marston.

But Samsen was also upset at having fallen down eleven times in the National City motel room where Skelly had deposited him after the surgery.

Evidently, the floor of the motel room was uneven because of a structural defect.

When contacted, a spokesperson for the proprietor, the Motel 6 Corporation, recently acquired by Yahoo, firmly denied this.

Samsen expired two days after the surgery from gangrene complicated by pneumonia, a blue ribbon medical panel testified.

Samsen died in the taxi en route to a Chula Vista hospital.

The taxi, piloted by a recently naturalized Somali, had gotten lost and arrived at the National City motel an hour and thirty-seven minutes late.

The cadaverous Jungian psychoanalyst with the dyed egg salad hair, Drake Marston, was to accompany his near-dead friend Samsen to the hospital.

When Samsen died, Marston instructed the cab driver, a slender, languid, café-au-lait-colored male named Ishmael, 34, to return to the National City motel.

Marston and Ishmael attempted to carry the dead amputee back into the motel room.

The record shows that Samsen twice slipped out of their grasp, the second time opening a gash on the left side of his already dead head.

Out of the gash issued blood and something else, a colorless thin stream, viscous.

After they finally laid the dead and bruised ampu-tee on the lumpy motel room bed and turned on the air conditioning, Marston dialed 911.

Just before the trial started, the former Dr. Skelly pleaded guilty to nine counts of practicing medicine without a license.

All the counts dealt with the eight transsexuals who were to testify but at the last minute were pre-vented from testifying, presumably because of a dream, fantasy, epiphany, vastation, visitation the judge ex-perienced after ingesting a dram of single malt Irish whisky.

Not Jameson as alleged, but Bushmills.

Damian Skelly faces six-and-a-half years in prison on each charge.

**

Ernesto "Che" Guevara's Christ-like portraits have been used to inspire leftist revolutionaries around the world.

Now, in an unprecedented interface of advertis-ing, politics and Christianity, Britain's churches are using Che's image to arouse interest in Jesus.

"We are trying to get away from the image of Jesus as a swishy bloke in a white nightie with a halo," explained Chaz Blofeld of the HHC&L advertising agency.

The result: Thousands of black-and-red billboards dotting the UK, from London to Edinburgh to Belfast to the outermost reaches of this once-proud Anglican island.

The billboard features Che Guevara, the bearded Marxist revolutionary, in a red beret, but without the Cuban cigar, morphed into Jesus wearing a crown of thorns.

The caption underneath reads:

Meek & Mild.
Cool too.
Discover the real Jesus.
At a Church near you.

The ads have drawn outrage from conservatives in the churches and from members of the political elite who claim that using a violent communist atheist to promote Jesus verges on blasphemy.

"A travesty of the gospel message," protested an editorial in Wednesday's *Daily Mail* tabloid.

"It is hard not to despair when churchmen can promote such offensive, dishonest and ignorant rubbish.

"Of course Christ was a revolutionary.

"His message today is as challenging and unsettling as ever.

"But he never planted bombs or executed his adversaries.

"His whole ministry was a repudiation of hatred and violence," the editorial said.

"Indeed, the central message of the gospels is the redeeming power of love."

The Christian advertising executives who dreamed up the campaign remained unmoved by the criticism.

They insist that their critics miss the point by focusing on Guevara the man instead of Guevara the revolutionary symbol.

Ad man Blofeld elaborated: "The New Testament is like an action video.

"It is violent, sensual, comical, revolutionary, fiercely angry.

"Filled to the brim with larger-than-life heroes and villains.

"It is almost never gentle, meek and mild, despite all of the poetry."

The highly controversial ads were commissioned by the Churches Advertising Network, or CAN, which represents the major Christian denominations of Britain.

The Reverend Quentin Ambrose of CAN asserts that the billboard advertisement was meant to make people reconsider Jesus, not abandon him.

"Jesus was a revolutionary symbol in his time and certainly more revolutionary than anyone who has lived since," he said.

"But the appeal of Jesus has diminished markedly in recent years.

"That is a fact and it must be rectified."

Hence the casting of the charismatic Che Guevara as Jesus.

But although Guevara undoubtedly is a symbol, he also was a man.

Ernesto "Che" Guevara, native of Argentina and a medical doctor, helped Fidel Castro overthrow Cuban dictator Fulgencio Batista on January 1, 1959, before moving on to try to spread communist ideology and revolution in third world countries on several continents.

He failed abysmally, was betrayed by fellow communists, and was executed in Bolivia in October 1967.

After his death, two photographs of Guevara became world famous.

One was a portrait of him in a beret, with uplifted eyes reflecting an unseen source of light.

The other was a photograph of the dead Guevara, eyes partially open and body laid out, looking uncannily like artistic representations of Jesus.

Each of the portraits has been accused of being doctored.

Nonetheless, the first portrait, taken by Cuban photographer Alberto Korda, helped turn Guevara into a martyr and icon for a generation of youthful leftists in the 1960s and '70s, from

Berkeley to Berlin,
Columbia to Calcutta,
Mexico City to Madrid,
Paris to Prague,
Kent State to Katmandu.

The Korda photograph showed up on T-shirts, key chains, posters, condom wrappers, toilet paper, and countless other items of kitsch and *objets d'art*.

It currently appears on Cuban currency and billboards throughout the island fiefdom.

(Incidentally, Korda, who recently died, insisted that he never received a peso for his Che Guevara, ranked as the best-selling photograph in the First World, having overtaken the previous leader: the 1955 promotional photo for *The Seven Year Itch* of Marilyn Monroe, half-standing, half-kneeling on a subway grating, her willowy white dress blown up around her thighs.)

Now, just as Christmas, Jesus's birthday, has returned to officially atheist Cuba, Che Guevara's image is being used for a variety of unrevolutionary purposes elsewhere.

Last year, the Polish-born Pope, John Paul II, made his maiden visit to Castro's Cuba, ushering in a new era of rapprochement between the Caribbean communist stronghold and the Vatican.

And last year, Christmas became an official holiday for the first time in Cuba since 1969, although the communist government warned its citizens against focusing on commercialism at the expense of spirituality.

What happens if individual Cubans choose to defy the edicts?

Presumably they will be shot or hanged or gassed or shipped to Miami.

Meanwhile, the Smirnoff vodka company in Britain, noting the controversial success of the Che-as-Jesus billboards, recently launched an advertising campaign using Guevara's image to sell alcoholic beverages.

Guevara, the fiery, cigar-smoking Latin revolutionary, is being used to promote "hot and fiery" spirits.

That Guevara was a severe asthmatic and teetotaler is nowhere alluded to.

Both the Smirnoff and the churches' ads were created by the latest computer technology.

Overlaying the Korda image of Che Guevara is a painting of Jesus that ad executives Chaz Blofeld and Trevor Wick of the Christian ad agency GDD&D appropriated from the Internet.

"These billboards are sacrilegious," declared Sir Hugh Peale-Somerset, a former Tory member of Parliament and sponsor of the Conservative Christian Fellowship.

"Jesus was perfect.

"It is grossly sacrilegious to liken him to a communist murderer like Che Guevara.

"I feel extremely strongly about this, and those who are responsible should be excommunicated straightaway."

Meg Winnecote, a Tory member of Parliament, tidily summed up the anti-billboard position: "We should be modeling ourselves on Christ, not modeling Christ on us."

The conservative *Mirror* tabloid ran a full-page photo of the controversial billboard under the headline "Chesus Christ."

The article accompanying the photo was highly critical of the billboard campaign.

The *Mirror* announced later that they had sold more copies of the "Chesus" issue than any other issue on record.

Ad man Blofeld dismissed the criticism. He said: "We are frankly not interested in appealing to fuddy-duddies and church reactionaries who are in point of fact responsible for moving people away from Christ."

Blofeld and Wick are the same pair that orchestrated a similarly controversial campaign two years ago called "Bad Hair Day."

That one, also featured on billboards nationwide, carried the caption:

Like a Virgin.
You've just given Birth.
And now three Kings have shown up.
One of whom is black as the Ace of Spades.
Find out the Happy ending at a Church near you.

Statistics indicate that the "Bad Hair Day" campaign did increase attendance at churches nationwide.

However, after six months the attendance not only decreased but fell beneath where it had been at the start of the campaign.

Blofeld, Wick and others insist that massive, ongoing advertising should be a fixture of church policy, as in the private sector.

"To pretend that the church somehow transcends the pulls and tugs of the real world is an illusion," ad man Blofeld said.

But for the ads to be effective they must be, in Blofeld's words, "boldly imaginative, audacious, unceasing."

"Like radiation therapy applied to a malignant tumor," Wick elaborated.

"Because Godlessness is a form of malignancy, which if untreated, will metastasize fast and relentlessly."

Regarding the "Chesus" campaign, Blofeld and Wick, whose team is called Christians in Media (CIM), claim to have donated their time without recompense.

"Except for a nominal per diem," ad man Wick clarified.

"And all we got for our pains was a few quid and a lot of flak," Blofeld added with a rueful grin, displaying uneven rows of very small beige teeth.

Nameless Moroccan 12 Stories Up

In this city renowned for its bad guys and bad news, something good happened Wednesday in downtown Los Angeles.

As a crowd stood transfixed, Johnny Childress, bailiff, morphed into Johnny Childress, hero, talking a suicidal man off a 12th-story ledge.

The drama, which began to unreel at about 11:40 a.m. and ended with the man being committed to psychiatric care, brought the busy lunchtime sidewalks to a standstill for more than an hour around the Los Angeles County Courthouse at First and Hill Streets.

On a deeper level, it also offered a case study in how real people respond to a real crisis.

Los Angeles County bailiff Johnny Childress was patrolling the first floor of the courthouse when he was radioed up to the 12th floor, where the cafeteria was located.

Someone, he was told, had thrown a pair of old pants from the cafeteria balcony.

Childress figured it was probably a homeless man. The homeless tend to do unpredictable things.

But when Childress got to the 12th-floor balcony he found a Moroccan with skinny, hairy legs, wearing dirty jockeys, a Snoop Doggy Dog T-shirt and a Dodgers baseball cap turned back to front.

He also wore outmoded Keds-brand black and white high-top sneakers, which looked comical with his skinny, hairy legs and jockeys.

He looked about 30 but could have been five years younger or ten years older.

He was standing, arms outstretched, on the lip of the concrete ledge.

"I said, 'Hey, bro. What's goin' down?'" Childress recalled.

"I figured I'd just order him off the ledge and that'd be it."

Instead the dark-skinned Moroccan turned and stared at the bailiff, his black eyes raw with tears.

"Don't come any closer," he pleaded.

Far below, a crowd had gathered.

Five fire engines rumbled to a stop, lights flashing.

Twelve LAPD cars, sirens whining and burping, screeched to a halt.

News helicopters, each with its network affiliate logo displayed, buzzed overhead.

On the courthouse steps a homeless man, who called himself Shabazz, offered regular updates to passersby.

"Yawl think he homeless.

"He ain't homeless," Shabazz the homeless man informed bystanders, as he rattled a Styrofoam cup for spare change.

"But don't make no dif neither way.

"He doomed.

"Cuz Lord say a soul ain't your own to take away."

At bailiff headquarters, Childress's bosses tried to summon the county sheriff's regular crisis negotiators, only to be told that they were attending a day-long retreat in Santa Monica, sponsored by Ruger International.

After the sheriff and deputies had contracted to use the Ruger 9mm semi-automatic as their official sidearm, Ruger convened retreats twice yearly.

What do folks do at the retreat? I don't know and I'm not sure I want to know.

Meanwhile, valuable time was passing.

With each second it became clear that Childress was the only soul to whom the deranged Moroccan would communicate.

At the man's insistence, three firefighters were ordered to back away from the ledge, leaving only Johnny Childress on the balcony.

With two video cameramen skulking in the doorway.

"I said, 'You don't want to do this,'" Childress recalled.

But the Moroccan was a font of despair.

He had lost the people he loved.

He was alone.

He was very tired.

He was scared.

In a rush of sorrow, he narrowed his eyes and murmured a prayer, or chant, in a strange language.

Then he dangled one sneakered foot over the edge.

"Get your foot back where it was!" Childress commanded.

"Get it back.

"Right now."

Startled, the man stopped short while Childress, thinking fast, peppered him with questions:

Did he have a family?

Did he root for the Dodgers?

Did he surf the Net?

Did he like hot dogs?

The Moroccan thought Childress meant actual dogs.

"I don't like dogs," the man answered.

"I like cats."

"I have a real nice cat," Childress told him.

"Sleeps with my dog."

Childress described the cat: a black, white and grey short hair with white boots, a white stripe on its nose and long white whiskers . . .

Childress talked rapidly, because at every pause the Moroccan would seem to remember his despondency, narrow his eyes and announce:

"This is it."

In the background, the two video cameramen inched ever closer.

The L. A. sun was now directly overhead.

You could sense it through the smog but you could not see it.

In the noonday heat, the man took off his Dodgers baseball cap and dangled it over the side.

Childress asked: "Do you believe in God?"

The Moroccan did not respond.

Far below, in the courtyard of the William Randolph Hearst Pavilion, a crowd of city workers was setting up balloon-bedecked booths for a ride-share fair.

Vainly, they tried to promote carpooling while simultaneously gazing at the man on the ledge.

Among the onlookers a conversation began.

Not a cynical conversation, as in previously recorded instances where bystanders wagered on whether a person would jump.

"How sad. To have no hope," a courthouse secretary in her nametag murmured.

"Maybe he just got fired," a man in his yellow chauffeur uniform said.

"Or his wife divorced him."

"Or he couldn't pay his rent."

"He looks like an Arab."

"What happened to his pants?"

"What they oughta do is throw him a big lasso," said a 38-year-old courthouse courier with a cleft palate.

"What I'd do," a woman with a juror's tag chimed in, "is go up in the building across the street and shoot him with one of those beanbag things, just to knock him back off the edge.

"Then I'd snatch him."

"If I could, know what I'd do?" a young man with a shaved head and tongue stud said.

"I'd take the balloons off of these booths and loft them to him, then he could just kinda float to the ground."

Twelve stories above, Johnny Childress gauged the distance between himself and the Moroccan.

What if he lunged for the guy's knees?

Would it work?

Too risky.

Except as a last resort.

The man said he was so tired.

So scared.

Childress assured him that he didn't have to worry.

There were deputies around to keep him safe.

The man met his eyes.

Could he get that in writing?

In a "promissory note" from Childress himself?

So the bailiff pulled out his notebook from his back pocket, licked his fingers and wrote: "I, Johnny Childress, Bailiff, promise to protect you, no matter what."

He used a capital "B" for Bailiff because he had pride in his work.

His work was law enforcement. To protect and serve.

Under the law.

Johnny Childress tore out the promissory note and held it out to the man, reckoning that if the man reached for it, he would grab his hand and pull him back.

But the man did not reach for it.

He kept repeating how afraid he was.

"I'll stand over your bed and guard you," Childress told the man.

"I'll protect you even when you sleep."

The Moroccan began to weep.

Then he started to pray hard and fast in his strange language.

Childress shouted to the man: "You are praying to God.

"God loves you.

"But God does not love folks that kill themselves.

"Suicides.

"This is the time to come down!

"I'm going to step toward you and give you my hand.

"**Will you take my hand?**"

On the ground far below, the crowd fell silent as the man stared at Childress without responding.

Everything appeared to slow up and come into focus.

Like fine tuning a large-screen TV.

Or accessing a site on the Internet.

www.namelesmoro.com

After what seemed like an ungodly time, the man took a step to the side and, trembling, held out his hand.

Johnny Childress clasped it with a powerful grip.

Everyone, except for the two video cameramen, smiled.

And down below, in Hearst Pavilion, everyone clapped their hands and smiled.

"Thank God," a woman in a cranberry jumpsuit said.

"Thank God."

Slurry

Bugs

Sonny Boy Nuñez, a medical riddle who inexplicably scratched himself to the point of self-mutilation and who was the center of an ambitious and briefly famous attempt to attain an independent life for a profoundly disabled individual, died Wednesday at a health care facility in the Bronx.

He was 25 and was living in Washington Heights, within sight of Yankee Stadium.

He was a lifelong Yankee fan and when he was six was visited in the children's ward by the great Mickey Mantle, who had a hangover but was nonetheless friendly to the children, if a bit distracted.

The cause of Sonny Boy's death was infection of the blood and spine, his parents said.

For reasons no one in the medical establishment professed to understand, Sonny Boy felt as if a million bugs crawled just under his skin.

To quiet his torment, he scratched himself so insistently that he ripped open his skin, even though he was a New York Rican who fell within the range of average intelligence and was fully aware of the damage he was inflicting.

I say "within the range of average intelligence," but how reliable are those standard IQ tests in any case?

At the very least, they are weighted against the collective consciousness of colored people.

Since the age of five, Sonny Boy was marooned in institutions, including one "sanatarium" that gave him electroshocks as part of its behavioral therapy regime.

Modalities once thought primitive, even barbaric, have made a comeback: notably electroshock and psychosurgery, a millennial synonym for lobotomy.

As he grew older, Sonny Boy desperately longed for a commonplace life like everyone else's.

As he once put it: "I want to have my own pad where I can turn my Santana disks up as loud as I want and have friends over."

In 1994, a small South Bronx social service agency, Job's Path, began a tortuous effort to answer his wishes and thereby to test the possibilities for the most shunned of the developmentally disabled.

In November 1996, the agency managed to move him into his own studio apartment in Washington Heights, the second floor of a pre-World War II building on 155th Street, just west of Amsterdam Avenue.

The efforts to gain his release and his first year of independent living were chronicled in a Fox TV special called "Sonny Boy's Blues," which, however, drew lower ratings than anticipated, probably because it was foolishly paired against Monday Night Football on ABC, which just happened to be featuring the Dallas Cowboys and Oakland Raiders.

Nonetheless, the Fox TV special thrust Sonny Boy into the limelight and generated a wide, if brief, interest in his case.

Sonny Boy was a diminutive young man, alternately sardonic and endearing, heavily scarred from his assaults on himself.

He was born in the South Bronx on Valentine's Day in 1973.

His parents, Dolly and Oscar Nuñez, found themselves depleted in their struggle to care for him.

Oscar worked as a chef's aide in a Cuban/Chinese restaurant in Chelsea, while Dolly was a clerk in a dry cleaning shop on Columbus Avenue.

Sonny Boy had an extraordinarily high tolerance for pain and would break his bones and rip off his toenails as well as scratch himself virtually to a bleeding pulp.

On the Fox special he was displayed furiously scratching, then banging his head against a stone wall in Morningside Park, which is south of Washington Heights.

He sustained a serious concussion.

That is, the stunt man standing in for the young Italian actor who represented Sonny Boy sustained a serious concussion on the Fox special.

Exhausted as much as heartbroken, Sonny Boy's parents reluctantly placed him in an institution, always hopeful that one day he would get out.

Finally he did, after 14 years of internment.

The mayor of New York elected to do what other cities had successfully done, namely release variously disabled patients into the street and transform the institutions and halfway houses into cash-crop residences.

Sonny Boy was one of several thousand released by the mayor's directive.

Once on his own, Sonny Boy experienced sharp mood swings, but he also made pronounced progress.

The first year in his Washington Heights apartment, he got a part-time job at a video store and took driving lessons.

He gained enough control of his impulse to scratch to go to movies and stores and baseball games unaccompanied by any of the three aides assigned to him.

He was on medication, of course.

One of the three aides, Sonny Boy's favorite, was a 30-year-old Filipino martial arts expert named Cato, who was also a medical technician, website designer and sometime bouncer.

Though Sonny Boy didn't scratch as violently as before, he still continued to scratch.

In December 1997, a leg infection brought on by his scratching sent him to a hospital and nearly killed him.

But then he made a remarkable recovery and returned to independent life.

He even entered a shuffleboard tournament in East Harlem.

However, the infection persisted.

It invaded his bones and spine.

When he was hospitalized in February, his legs became paralyzed.

At the end of July, in need of full-time nursing care, he was moved into the Terence Cardinal Cooke Health Care Center in the northeast Bronx, which is where he died.

Interestingly, he died five months before the date the Fox TV special dramatized him dying; one of the two dates had to be wrong.

His last word, purportedly, was "grace."

This was disputed by Fox who claimed it was "mace," a commentary on local police strong-arm methods with which he was substantially in agreement, an obedient citizen, despite his color, social status, emotional fragility and fatal scratching, according to Fox.

Cato cried at being separated from him.

Sonny Boy is survived by his parents and his younger brother, Benny.

The family is being consoled by a grief counselor.

Rocks

Alone and barefoot, a man reportedly pelted officers with baseball-sized rocks he carried in a pouch by his belt.

Until he was fatally shot by a border patrol agent, ending the two-hour confrontation yesterday near the California-Mexico border.

A border patrol agent and a caretaker for the Sweetwater Authority were treated at local hospitals after being struck by rocks in the chest and back.

Sheriff's homicide Sgt. Byron Sprague said the incident began at 6:45 a.m. yesterday near Loveland Reservoir on Japatul Road, southeast of Alpine, as caretaker Mike Muntz was opening the reservoir for fishermen, who pay a yearly fee to underwrite the cost of stocking the reservoir with game fish.

Muntz noticed something that looked like a metal box on the ground and went to investigate.

Suddenly he began getting hit by rocks, said Danny Bostig, deputy operations manager for the authority, which provides much-needed water for National City, Chula Vista and Bonita.

Muntz radioed for help, but not before being struck in the small of the back with a rock.

Within minutes a border patrol agent drove up and his camo-green Ford Expedition was barraged by rocks, one of which shattered a rear window, according to Sgt. Sprague.

Backup force was summoned.

The suspect fled west along Japatul Road, Sgt. Sprague said, alternately walking and running—picking up more rocks along the way—before veering south onto a dirt path toward the reservoir.

Three sheriff's deputies, a San Diego Police Department dog team, and a half-dozen border patrol agents arrived to aid in the search.

The officers were fit and muscular; an estimated 73 percent of them ingest steroids to build muscle mass.

It is important to note that these steroids are (as of this writing) 100 percent legal, the same brand that Mark McGwire and Sammy Sosa have used.

The border patrol agents scoured the brush nearest the road, but after a few minutes they found tracks pointing south into the foothills of the Chocolate Mountains.

Trained to distinguish various kinds of prints, the agents had little trouble following the marks left by the shoeless man with his pouch full of rocks, said Border Patrol spokesperson Maria Villareal-Deutsch.

However, the police dogs were of little use.

"It's very dense, thick brush, chaparral," Villareal-Deutsch explained.

"The dogs simply weren't able to negotiate the brush and follow the tracks."

After about an hour's search, border patrol trackers finally caught up with the suspect.

"Throughout the pursuit, the tracking agents were shouting commands to freeze, to stop throwing rocks, identifying themselves in English and in Spanish," Sgt. Sprague said.

"Nowhere in this encounter did the suspect respond verbally whatsoever to them," Sgt. Sprague said.

Instead the suspect continued to reach into his pouch and throw rocks.

"Some of the agents were struck by the rocks," Sgt. Sprague said.

At one point, while throwing rocks, the suspect "began advancing toward the tracking agents in a menacing fashion," according to the Sheriff's department.

"One of the agents was struck in the chest by a large rock," Sgt. Sprague said.

Even though the agent wore a bulletproof vest, the rock "stung."

All border patrol agents are issued bulletproof "Kevlar vests."

In response the agent shot the suspect with his Austrian-made Glock 9mm.

He emptied his clip which holds 17 rounds, 14 of which found their target.

This was routine procedure, Villareal-Deutsch explained.

Agents began administering first aid to the suspect on the spot.

They summoned paramedics.

The paramedics reached the man while his heart was beating, but it was too late.

"The suspect died at the scene," Sgt. Byron Sprague said.

The dead suspect was identified only as "a 6-foot Hispanic."

Which is larger than Hispanics tend to grow.

Except that Mexicans living adjacent to the US are subject to US nutritional practices and legal steroid supplements, hence grow larger and more muscular than their compatriots in the interior.

There was speculation that the suspect might have been a drug smuggler, a "coyote" (migrant smuggler), or an illegal immigrant.

Nothing about his identity or background could be confirmed as of yesterday.

Although the Sheriff's Department was in charge of the scene after the shooting, the actual investigation will be conducted by the FBI, which will forward its report to the US Attorney in San Diego.

The US Attorney's Office, rather than the county District Attorney, will determine whether the shooting was justified, Sgt. Sprague explained.

With a small army of exceptionally fit county and federal law enforcement officers, backed by a border patrol helicopter, trying to piece together what happened, Sgt. Byron Sprague did not try to hide his bewilderment.

"It just doesn't make any sense to me," he said, referring to the dead, rock-throwing suspect.

"I've seen a lot of strange stuff in my 11-and-a-half years down here by the border.

"But what he did did not seem to be reasonable behavior."

Germs

Anyone who wants to strike a city by spraying anthrax from a plane would need a crop duster with custom-built nozzles that could accommodate germ particles between 1 and 5 microns in size.

Particles smaller than that would not have enough mass to float in the air properly.

Larger particles would not be properly absorbed into the lungs.

To generate high casualties, the anthrax would have to be turned into freeze-dried anthrax, which can yield potencies of 100 percent.

Except that freeze-drying requires complicated, costly equipment that can handle the spores in air-tight containers.

Only government-sponsored bio-weapon programs, such as Iraq's or North Korea's, are likely to have such equipment.

Anthrax is simpler to handle in a wet form called slurry.

But the potency of this wet material is typically 10 percent to 15 percent.

Employing slurry, a low-tech terrorist could efficiently assault an institutional headquarters with a hand-held sprayer.

POST-APOC

Dr. Death

And now, please put your virtual hands together for Dr. Death.

[Applause]

Dr. Death, welcome. Sit right down there next to Charo.

[Charo makes to hug the doctor, who pulls back violently]

I don't like anyone's hands on me.

She's not anyone Doc; she's Charo, the original coochie-coochie girl. She sang and jiggled with Cugat. She had extensive reconstructive surgery. She's your bona fide TV and Internet talk-show bimbo.

Never mind.

**[The doctor sits on the absinthe green leather sofa
and crosses his thin legs]**

They call you Dr. Death but your real name is Jack
Kevorkian?

Correct.

No one has ever called you Jack the Ripper, I sup-
pose.

[Whistles, laughter]

Just yourself.

I see that you're dressed as you always dress: old
ratty cardigan, Salvation Army trousers, black, scuffed
workshoes. The makeshift clothes and that stark grey
crewcut are sort of your signature, right, Doc?

[Kevorkian does not respond]

How many folks have you euthanized?

Euthanized is inaccurate. I have provided assis-
tance for suicides. You want the number? One hundred thirty-two.

[Applause, loud whistling]

Whoa! If you were a serial killer you'd hold the
world record.

The world these very sick people inhabited had
already killed them. Their hearts beat but they were,
for all practical purposes, dead.

[The host is glancing through the publicity material]

And you're not just a medical doctor. You taught yourself how to play the . . . harpsichord, you are a gifted painter, you speak a bunch of languages—

Just hobbies. I am a pathologist.

[Scattered applause]

About your paintings, they were described as "strikingly well-executed, stark, surreal, and demented or hilarious, depending on your point of view." Is that an accurate description?

Couldn't say. I painted some canvases to raise money for my cause.

Where are they now?

The originals were stolen. I don't want to discuss it. I no longer paint.

Well, you're obviously skilled with your hands. You constructed your own death machine, right?

I didn't have much choice, did I?

How did you build it?

You mean where did I find the materials? The hardware store, garage sales, flea markets. I used an old lawn mower motor.

Sort of like Dr. Frankenstein, right?

Not right. Frankenstein is fiction. I'm talking about harsh reality.

[Loud boos, then laughter, scattered applause]

You even named it—this death machine. What's it called, Doc?

Thanatron.

That's Latin—

Greek. It means death machine.

Makes sense. It says here that you've been fascinated with death since you were a kid, performing amateur autopsies on anything dead you could lay your hands on—

Is that what it says?

Right here. I guess you didn't write it yourself, huh?

Nope.

Though you were fascinated with dissection and death, one of your boyhood friends, Rick Dakesian, a fellow Armenian, says that your first love was baseball. That true?

Well, that's what it says on the printout.

Rick Dakesian says that not only could you recite any major league player's batting average, but you knew the pitchers' earned run averages. You even knew their heights and weights and when they were born. Rick said that you actually wanted to be a baseball announcer, but that your parents disapproved. That's amazing.

Why?

Because baseball is fun, and fun ain't exactly the first thing that comes to mind when the name Dr. Death is mentioned. You still follow baseball?

No. Between my work and answering moronic questions from Internet hosts, I have no time for games.

[Boos, scattered hisses, laughter]

Your work is of course death in many of its guises, and it is clear that you've attained a comfort level in what you're doing. You're familiar with the bumper sticker: "Death Sucks," right?

What's the question?

The big D. Death. You don't seem to be scared shitless of it like the rest of us earthlings.

Billions have died on this depleted planet of ours, okay? The dead must wonder, in their vegetable way, what the fuss is about. After all, how excruciating can nothingness be?

[pause]

You're asking me, Doc?

You have something to add?

[Charo chimes in]

Death. I no frightened of eet.

[Doctor Death addresses Charo from the opposite end of the long leather sofa]

So you expect to end up in heaven?

Me? Jes. I go up there.

[The host]

What about you, Doctor Death? Will you end up in heaven? Or will those 132 assisted suicides stand in your way?

What stands in my way are pious fools and cowardly bureaucrats.

You've murdered—that is, assisted—132 would-be suicides and not been prosecuted. What else do you want?

I want to transfuse blood from a freshly dead cadaver to a human in need. With his permission, I want to put the condemned criminal in a deep, drugged sleep, conduct experiments on his body; then, when the experiments are completed, I want to execute the prisoner humanely, by injection.

[Catcalls, loud yodeling]

I want to videotape the eyes of a person passing from life to death. I want to remove the stomach, pancreas and kidneys from a full term infant born with severe spina bifida, paraplegia and hydrocephalus.

Why? Why do you want to do those things?

Think for a minute. Because you're an Internet host in a shiny suit with surgically repaired features and a hair weave shouldn't prevent you from thinking.

Thanks a lot, Doc. Okay, you're removing organs from live people—

Condemned people. Hopeless cases. The irreparably doomed.

Got it. You're experimenting on hopeless cases for the sake of science.

Correct. That great abstraction Science.

[Mocking hoots and whistles, scattered applause]

You've made more than your share of enemies among fellow scientists. Is that a fair statement, Dr. Death?

You say "scientists" as if it's a privileged category. Scientists, like lawyers and corporate managers, and Internet hosts, tend to be cowards. Afraid to deviate from the culture that rewards their cowardice. When challenged, they justify their cowardice with lies and character assassination.

Okay. I'd like to quote something you wrote: "We squander priceless opportunities to study ourselves and our living brains, as well as new ways to make us wiser, healthier and happier. We snuff out lives of criminals eager to make amends by donating their organs and helping science unlock some of nature's deepest secrets." Those are your words?

Yes. I also said that if there are willing condemned criminals, there must be willing non-criminals who have opted for euthanasia. I would perform the same experiments on those suicidal humans.

Are you talking only about physical disabilities, or do you include folks that are suicidal because of their mental condition?

If their suffering is primarily emotional and they have been unable to receive adequate care, then, yes, I would assist them. And, with their permission, I would experiment on them.

But isn't that immoral, Doctor?

What's immoral, and almost intolerably banal, is your moronic interrogation.

[Whistles, loud applause, one elaborate yodel]

The one word that's always used when talking about right to death campaigns is compassion. Would you describe yourself as a compassionate person, Dr. Death?

I'll leave those descriptions to others.

As long as they are not moronic, right?

Obviously.

Well, here is one of those others. And he is not moronic, even by your rigorous standards. A Nobel laureate in biophysics. He had this to say: "Whether Kevorkian's obsessions benefit humankind matters less to him than the rush—the almost orgasmic rush—he seems to get from handling and fantasizing about handling cadavers." Comment?

I already commented on sanitized scientists whose cowardice is rewarded. This so-called Nobel laureate is a prime example of that.

You are a very angry man, Doc. Don't you think that Dr. Death here is an angry man, Charo?

Jes. But I like heem. He help people that don have no theen.

[Whistling, laughter, one raucous Bronx cheer]

You've got a fan, Doc.

I'm not an entertainer.

You're not? What about *Slimmeriks and Demi-Diet?* **To the Internet audience:** In 1975 Doctor Death authored a humorous diet book by that name. **To Kevorkian**: Wouldn't you call that entertainment?

Have you read the book?

Can't say that I have.

Read it. You might profit from it and extend your life. The gist of it, without the limericks, is don't smoke, avoid milk products, exercise moderately, eat as often as you need to, but only half the amount. Leave half of every plate uneaten.

That's it?

Basically. Without the humorous part—the limericks.

Can you recite one of those limericks for our virtual audience?

"A life of profane deglutition / Can end in a grave condition / How you consumed / Cannot be entombed / Thanks to the brave mortician."

[Puzzled laughter, mocking whistles, two ear-splitting Bronx cheers]

You hear that, Charo? Did you like Dr. Death's humorous limerick?

Jes. I do. Bery much.

Charo seems to be on your wavelength, Doc. Can't say that I am.

You may be soon if you keep eating, boozing, wearing that strong cologne and obsessing about sex.

[Hoots, applause]

Give me a break! What do you have against sex?

Sex is sex. Obsessing about it or anything else will compromise your health. I wouldn't want you to die before your time.

But if I happened to drop dead you would harvest my organs?

Only with your permission.

[Loud, shrill, extended catcall]

Speaking of sex: You've never married. How come? Never found Ms. Right? Or is there an issue—

My work.

Your work is death. You're married to death, is that it, Doc?

So are we all. You're an even bigger fool than I gave you credit for if you can't see that.

[pause]

Okay. Let's say euthanasia is finally permitted and becomes the law of the land. Would that satisfy you?

No. Such a death, no matter how serene, serves no constructive purpose beyond the bleak aim of extinguishing life.

You want to be able to conduct experiments on the corpses . . .

As I've been saying, I would conduct experiments on the cadavers and especially on the would-be cadavers, while he or she was still alive, but asleep of course, drugged beyond pain.

[Applause, two Bronx cheers, scattered yodeling]

Shoot. Looks like we've run out of time. Sorry about that, Doc. We have about thirty seconds. If you had a single word to say to our planet-wide virtual audience, what would it be?

[Kevorkian does not respond; the host inquires]

Have you gone on Letterman yet?

Who?

David Letterman.

Glasses, gap-toothed, with the arrogant manner?

Er. That's him.

He's next. I think tomorrow. Need to check my
calendar.

[pause]

Awesome. Well, that's a wrap. Doctor Death, it's
been a . . . learning experience. You're a very, very in-
eresting human. From now on, whenever I see that
bumper sticker "Death Sucks", I'll think of you in your
funky cardigan and scuffed workshoes and be reminded that death, the big D, doesn't suck. It's us, the
living-breathing folks, that, so to speak, suck death—
and profit immeasurably from its grave restrictions.

Thanks a bunch, Doc. You're far from the dud I
heard you were. You're a little weird of course, and
sort of foul tempered, but you're actually a pretty cool
guy. You've done it your way, and we all can appreci-
ate that.

And you all out there in virtual land, from Pluto to
Pensacola, from Uranus to Hyannis, from Tel Aviv to
Texarkana, please give a little love to Doctor Death.

**[Whistles, hoots, yodels, catcalls, loud applause,
Bronx cheers, two or three shrieks of pain. Charo
blows the doctor a kiss, which he does not ac-
knowledge. He rises from the sofa, doesn't wave
to the virtual audience, looks to the right, then
left, which is where he heads, moving a little stiff-
legged in his crewcut, plain shoes, ratty cardigan
and Salvation Army trousers, offstage]**